DANI ELIAS

Build with Me

A Small Town, Grumpy/Sunshine Romance

To Ebony

I'm ADDING THIS BOOK
AS IT GIVES you SOME
BACK GROUND ON THE
Greenview MANOR HOTEL!

Sorry IT's THE OLD
COVER, BUT THE
STORY IS UNCHANGED!

Dan E

Editor: Sofia Artola Diaz

First edition

ISBN: 978-1-7393324-5-7

This book was professionally typeset on Reedsy.
Find out more at reedsy.com

Contents

Dedication	v
Content Warning	vii
Chapter 1	1
Chapter 2	9
Chapter 3	16
Chapter 4	23
Chapter 5	31
Chapter 6	36
Chapter 7	43
Chapter 8	50
Chapter 9	55
Chapter 10	63
Chapter 11	72
Chapter 12	77
Epilogue	84
WANT MORE?	89
THANK YOU	90
MORE FROM DANI ELIAS	91

Dedication

In loving memory of Snail Bail, who showed us all that we can thrive with the right support. (And that it's okay to get frisky with ourselves).

A cause close to my heart

My Fellside Mountain Rescue Series is about the men and women of a fictional group of volunteers risking their lives to help those in danger in the mountains. My characters may be fictional, but many mountain rescuers around the world do just this every day and they deserve our respect, our support and at the bare minimum our thanks.

Thank you!

Content Warning

Build with Me is a contemporary romance novella which includes scenes of a sexual nature. It is not a closed-door story.

This book also contains references to

- Violence and physical abuse
- Mental abuse
- Strong language

If any of this serves as a trigger for you, please decide if this is the book for you.

Finally, the books are set in the north of England and British English spelling is used throughout. That means a lot of times you'll find an "S" where you may expect a "Z". And our ass has an extra Rrrrr to it ;-). P.S. Spotted Dick is a dessert.

Chapter 1

Tommy

L oud laughter drifts over to me. I place my rucksack in the back of the Range Rover with the large Fellside Mountain Rescue logo on the side.

"Can you fucking cut it out and hurry up?" I yell in the direction of where the guys are gathering the gear. I am already late for a meeting with a supplier and I really don't need any further unnecessary delays.

How I have managed to combine my work with volunteering for FMR is sometimes a mystery, although it has become easier since Ella took over as my assistant. She uses some kind of magic or voodoo to keep business partners happy when I have to reschedule yet another meeting because some tourist has gotten themselves lost in the hills of Cumbria. Well, not magic really, but she cunningly hypes up my volunteer role with FMR, so much so that the person feels too guilty to complain, given that I am doing "such noble work". She even managed to get some of them to donate to FMR. She really is something special.

I untie my heavy mountaineering boots and slip my trainers

on. I find it easier to drive in my trainers. Another backpack drops into the boot of the car. *Thank fuck, they're finally ready to leave.*

"Want to tell me what's wrong with you today?" Alex asks. In between tying my shoelaces, I glance at him as he leans against the side of the Range Rover with his arms crossed in front of him. He is still wearing his FMR jacket and a beanie to protect him from the cold autumn air.

"Nothing. I just have a meeting."

"Mate, you always have a meeting. But that's never stopped you from having a laugh with us at the end of a mission before."

"It's an important one." *Not true.* It's just another laundry company that wants to try to convince me to send my linen to them.

Alex raises an eyebrow. Of course, he is not buying that shit, he knows me too well. Alex and I are the longest serving members of FMR in our unit. We both joined as volunteers at the same time; I was twenty-three and Alex was nineteen. When I was promoted to unit leader I insisted that Alex was part of my team. The only other guy left from those early days is Nick. Over the years we added Chris, Rob and Phil to our unit and those five have become my best friends. During a mission I am their boss, but the rest of the time we are just six lads having a laugh — if I'm not busy with work, that is.

Our latest member Suzie is currently not taking part in missions. She and Chris are expecting a baby and with all will in the world, there is no climbing for her now that she is in her third trimester.

Alex sits down on the edge of the boot. "I've drawn the short straw to find out what is wrong with you. So, if you want to get to your meeting in good time, you better spill."

I sigh and sit down next to him. "Fuck, I don't know, Alex. It's all getting a bit much." My fingers slide through my sweaty hair.

"Work and FMR?"

"Yes." It's only half the truth, but it is the truth.

"Why don't you take a break from FMR?" He is asking a valid question.

"Are you after my job?" I laugh trying to divert. Although we don't officially have a second in command at FMR, Alex is kind of my unofficial deputy. He is calm under pressure and all of the lads respect him and look up to him.

"Bollocks to that," he laughs. "But I am willing to help out a friend for a while."

"I don't really want to give it up and I promised my dad I wouldn't," I try to explain. My grandfather played a role in the formation of the first rescue team in Fellside in the 1940s. Later on, my dad joined him and both were Fellside Mountain Rescue volunteers until the day they died. It meant a lot to them. So much so that my dad made me swear I wouldn't give it up when he saw how much of my life I sacrificed for my business.

"Nobody is talking of you giving it up. Why don't you take a month or two off from being a leader? I'll sub for you and you can still join our missions. But it means you don't have to worry about all the paperwork and all that shit."

"You hate the paperwork."

"That's the kind of friend I am," he chuckles. I look out into the distance. I can see the roofs of Fellside from up here. Somewhere beyond is my hotel where I should be having coffee with some sales guy trying to get me to sign a contract right now.

"Are you sure?" Somehow it doesn't feel right in my guts. Call me a control freak, but it is like passing on my baby. One of my babies, the other being my hotel.

"Definitely. Oh, and we also think you need to get laid," he adds matter-of-factly before standing up and starting to sort some of the rope bundles into the plastic crate we keep in the back of the car.

"Fuck off," I push back but really, he is not wrong. The minute he says the words, the image of a brunette in a tight pencil skirt is conjured up in my mind.

"What's that look on your face?" Alex asks with a smirk.

"I don't know what you're talking about." I sound defensive and I know that I just made a big mistake. I busy myself removing climbing gear from my backpack. The guys driving the Range Rover back to the FMR Centre will tidy it all away. I have my car parked lower on the mountain so I can head straight back to my hotel.

"Fuck, Tommy, we have been friends for over fifteen years. I have only once seen that look on your face and that was back when the she-devil put her claws in you." I stiffen when he mentions my ex-girlfriend. I was infatuated with her until I found out that all she was after was my hotel.

"You are shagging someone."

"I am most definitely not." I might wish I would be, but it's definitely not going to happen.

"Even better, there's a woman you are seriously interested in." He points at me and a cheeky smile appears on his lips.

"No."

"Tommy, stop fucking around. Tell me. Who is she?"

"It doesn't matter. I'm not going after her."

Alex sits down on the boot again.

"Why not?"

4

"She works for me."

"Who works for you?" Nick steps up to us and puts the casualty bag next to the ropes.

"Nobody."

"Bit difficult to run a hotel without staff, mate," he laughs about his own joke but he stops when neither Alex nor me join in. Alex has his arms crossed in front of his chest and is just looking at me expectantly. *Well shit.* There is no way he's going to drop the topic. I ruffle my hair and blow out hard.

"My assistant Ella." The minute I say her name I feel the tightening in my guts I get every time I am close to her.

"You have the hots for your assistant?" Nick blurts.

"Yes, fuck, it's stupid. And no, before you ask, nothing can happen!" I point at both of them. Alex raises his hands in surrender.

"Mate, I haven't said anything. But tell me, why did you hire her?"

"I didn't. My HR manager did." After complaining to Anna for the hundredth time that I needed more help, she finally went out and hired an assistant for me. I should have been in the interviews but as usual I was too busy and I thought I could leave it to Anna. Truth be told, she did hire the best person for the job. It's not really Anna's fault that I don't have my dick under control.

"So, you didn't hire her because you fancied her?"

"Fuck no. I didn't even see her before she started with me. I wasn't in the interviews and I would never hire someone because of the way they look. And if you must know, she is amazing at her job."

"So, what's the problem?" Nick asks and then takes a bite from an apple he has pulled out of his rucksack.

5

"I can't hit on my assistant. It's wrong. It could also get me into all sorts of hot water if she's not interested and make me look like a creep. And I don't want to lose her as my assistant."

"So, instead, you just take your frustration out on everyone else," Nick remarks which makes Alex chuckle.

"Fuck, was I that bad?"

"I think Gordon Ramsey swears less in a week than you did in the last three hours."

"I didn't realise—"

"It's okay, mate. We've all been there, but fuck, talk to us." Alex slaps me on the shoulder. "And think about my offer."

I nod and pull the zip up on my jacket.

"And I would think again about if you want to give it a try with your assistant. Not everyone is like the she-devil," Nick adds before peeking past the car to where Chris and Phil are waiting. "It's safe to come. He's in a better mood."

* * *

Every time I drive up to the hotel and see the elegant sign saying Greenview Manor, I am amazed that this is all mine. I worked in the hotel trade all my life. I finished school when I was sixteen and started as an apprentice when the hotel still belonged to Mr Sinder. He encouraged me to spread my wings and learn the trade by working in some other hotels as well. I did a couple of ski seasons in Austria and one dreadful summer in an posh hotel in Tuscany. But I always knew I wanted to come back here. I started on reception and worked my way up to hotel manager. And when Mr Sinder decided to retire, I used the money I had inherited from my dad as well as a very sizeable mortgage to buy it and make it mine. I have spent the last five years improving the standard of the hotel, and last year we were voted the number one venue in the Lake District. The phones haven't stopped since and there is hardly a day when we are not at at least ninety percent occupancy.

I park my car in my designated parking spot in front of the hotel and lean back in my seat. *Fuck, I'm tired.* The call for this mission came at five this morning. It is now ten and I haven't even had breakfast yet.

Movement to the left catches my attention. *There she is, the angel that haunts my dreams.* Ella steps out from the front entrance in her usual business attire of pencil skirt and blouse. She and I are the only ones in the hotel that don't wear the uniform of black trousers and polo shirt, and I'm glad she doesn't. With her chestnut brown hair casually pinned up and her curves accentuated by that damn pencil skirt, she is a vision.

I take a deep breath before opening the door to my car and stepping out.

"Morning, Tommy," she greets me with a big smile.

"Morning," I mumble. Did I forget to mention that ever since she joined us, I have turned into a complete arsehole? It's a defence mechanism, I guess.

"I've moved your meeting with the new laundry company to tomorrow. Otherwise, you are free until lunch time when you are meeting with Simon from King's Travel," she rattles off and holds out a mug which I assume has coffee in it. I take it from her and flinch a little when our fingers touch. If she has noticed my reaction, she is not letting on.

"Thanks," I grunt. Ella just gives me a small smile and looks down at her tablet.

"You might want to take a shower—"

"That's exactly what I had planned, thank you. Have the

7

occupancy numbers ready for me when I come back down," I snap before taking a big gulp from the mug. *Fuck, that coffee is hot.* I feel it burning all the way down into my stomach and I try hard to not show the pain on my face.

"The numbers are already on your desk," she smirks and stalks off towards the hotel entrance. Before she pushes the door open, she turns to me. "Oh, and Tommy, the coffee is hot."

That little minx.

Chapter 2

Ella

T he heavy entrance door closes behind me with a loud thud. As Tommy is not in his usual suit, he'll take the staff entrance at the back to get into the building. I know him, he is too much of a professional to be caught by his guests in his FMR gear. Not that he isn't proud of his volunteering, but he has strict rules for the hotel and he would never break them.

"Tommy is back, so the heads of department meeting this afternoon will go ahead. Please let everyone know," I say to Lindsey, the young receptionist, as I pass the front desk. She nods but doesn't reply as an elderly couple approaches her.

I love this place. Tommy has done an incredible job in transforming the hotel. The great hall next to reception is definitely my favourite part. Stained glass windows in the ceiling, beautiful woodwork, a feature fireplace, and elegant furniture all create a sense of grandeur transporting you back to Victorian times.

The wooden staircase leading from the ground floor to the first floor creaks under my feet. Tommy seems to be extra grumpy again today. He is an enigma. He can be incredibly kind one minute and a big grouch the next. Only last week he went out and purchased an insane amount of baby gifts for one of the waitresses who had given birth to a baby boy. Most staff look up to him and consider him a great boss, the guests love him and, despite his busy life, he gives up his time to volunteer for FMR. Rumour has it that he can also be a fun guy especially when he hangs out with his friends, but I have yet to see this side. All he has been with me since I started was grumpy.

I asked Anna once if he wasn't happy with me and I guess she must have spoken with him because for a few days he was a little friendlier but now we are back to Lord Grumpiness. Don't get me wrong, he isn't mean to me (believe me, I had my share of viciousness directed at me when working in my family's firm). No, Tommy is like a grumpy teddy bear. I don't think he could harm a fly.

After I passed my probation, I became a little braver and when he gets too arsy, like just now, I do give back. I love the shocked look on his face when I stand up to him. He doesn't know what to do with himself in those situations and just mumbles something before retreating to his office. It makes me giggle every time.

I step into the small room just outside Tommy's office where my desk is and drop my tablet next to my laptop. Both rooms were originally Mr Bryant's study, the wealthy owner who built this place in the eighteen hundreds. Now they are two boring offices with magnolia walls and beige carpets. But the furniture is chunky and old, giving the room a little character. And Tommy's corner office has stunning views, on one side of the mountains and on the other of Lake Windermere.

I walk to the small coffee machine on the credenza. Tommy

doesn't allow himself much luxury, all his profits are reinvested on improving the hotel. But he insists on having one of those fancy coffee machines with capsules in the office. He prefers that brew even over the freshly made ones from the restaurant. I prepare everything so I only need to press the button when he comes down. He will want to have another cup after he was called out at five this morning; that's the time he texted me to let me know he would be late.

Tommy's small flat is in the attic of the hotel. He lives and breathes this hotel and he usually works seven days a week so staying on site makes sense for him. How he hasn't burnt out yet, I really don't know.

I glance at my phone where a message notification is blinking. Knots form in my tummy when I see who it is. I pick up the phone with shaking hands.

Lee: Just checking we are all set with the big boss.

I hesitate for a minute before replying to my brother.

Me: Of course. Your appointment is set for four p.m. on Tuesday as per my email.

Immediately the little moving dots appear and tell me that he is replying.

Lee: That's not what I meant. Have you been working him?
Me: What?
Lee: To make sure he hires us.
Me: He will choose whichever company is best.

My family has the most prestigious architecture company in the area but getting Tommy's hotel extension project would be a fantastic opportunity.

Lee: For fuck's sake, Ella, for once put the family first.
Me: I have! When I drew the plans for your proposal.

I throw my phone on my desk. Fear spreads through me. I shouldn't have said that. He is going to make me pay. I pick the phone up again.

Lee: You are lucky I'm not there.
Lee: You better make sure he likes YOUR plans as much as you think he will, because if we don't get this deal it's all your fault. And you wouldn't want me to tell him that you've been plotting behind his back. I thought you liked the job at that hotel.

I don't reply to Lee's message but my fear is replaced in parts by anger. I always put the family first. For five years I quietly worked in the background, creating design after design that secured project after project whilst my brother took credit for it. "It's for the family," I was told by Lee and by my dad.

Don't get me wrong, I am not a praise seeker but I would love recognition when I work hard. Eventually I had enough and decided to leave the family business. My brother, who always had a violent side, didn't take it well. I hid in Fellside whilst my bruises were healing. I couldn't really attend a job interview with a massive black eye.

I sent out CVs to different architecture firms in Cumbria but being a member of the Grange family meant that no other architecture firm would go anywhere near me. Whilst my dad's company had won many awards, within the industry the company was known for unfair business practices. My brother and my dad don't shy away from bribery or even threats and other dirty tricks but nobody has been able to prove it yet. Their bad reputation tainted my name as well.

When Lee eventually found me in Fellside (I still don't know how he did it), he tried to get me to come back with him. But I wasn't budging. My job here meant something to me, and I wasn't about to ditch it. Lucky for me, we were in a coffee shop and so he couldn't make a scene. He stormed off, and I stayed put for another hour, hoping he'd actually left, before I sneaked back to my flat.

I didn't hear from him again until a month or so later, when Tommy sent out a tender to architecture firms for the extension. I couldn't really stop him from including my family, as they are well known. Lee asked me to draw the plans for the extension. And now I am paying the price for not standing up to my family once again.

When I couldn't find a job as an architect, I applied for anything and everything just so I could stay in Fellside and I ended up at Greenview Manor. I love my job and I am the happiest I have been in a long time. Tommy is a handful, but the job is fun and interesting and I admire Tommy's business sense. He is incredible with people, except with me, and he deeply cares about the hotel.

If only he wouldn't make me nervous and giddy at the same time. Aside from being an amazing person he is incredibly attractive. I don't think there is a single female staff member who doesn't secretly fancy him. As of late he has become one of my favourite masturbation fantasies and I am pretty sure it is not okay to picture your boss giving you a good shafting almost every night. A small smile spreads on my lips and I can feel my cheeks heat up. No, I definitely don't want to lose this.

"Love, is Tommy here?" The voice of Ian brings me back to reality.

"He's getting changed, Chef," I reply and busy myself with printing some reports. I made the mistake on my first day to call Ian, the head chef, by his first name and was promptly put in my place by his sous-chef. It's ridiculous really. We even call Tommy by his first name. But when it comes to the kitchen staff, everyone thinks they are the next Monsieur Escoffier.

Ian leans against my desk and taps on the wood until I look at him.

"When can I take you out, love?" He asks in his thick Brummie accent.

"Ia...Chef, I told you before, I'm not interested." I give him my best stern look before returning my attention to my emails.

"Playing hard to get, are we? You know, I won't ask forever, I have other options." He gives me a cheesy grin. I very much doubt that he has many options and that has nothing to do with the fact that he always smells like chicken stock or that he tries to cover his bald patch by using way too much gel to hold his hair in place. No, it is all down to him being a creep. He is a brilliant chef which is why he is still here, but he has been warned a number of times by Anna.

"Ian, what are you doing here?" Tommy's voice booms through the office drawing both mine and Ian's attention to him. Yes, Tommy is allowed to call Ian by his first name. I would love to see someone tell him he has to call that creep Chef.

"Tommy, I've the menus for the VIP fundraiser."

"Leave them with Ella, I'll have a look at them this afternoon."

"Sure." There is an edge to Ian's voice. He hates it when

Tommy puts him in his place. "See you at the department meeting." He waves a goodbye and leaves my office.

"Was he inappropriate?" Tommy looks at me and for the first time I see something else than grumpiness staring back at me. He looks... concerned, maybe, but there seems to be something else.

"No," I laugh, "He's just Ian. I've forwarded you an email from the bank you need to look at, please."

"Sure." He slides his large hand over the smooth top of my desk before walking towards his office. "Ella, tell me if he bothers you." His eyes find mine. They are caring and have lost their usual hard edge. I forget to breathe and his concerned look warms my insides. I almost wish he would return to being a grump.

I give him a small smile and say, "Don't worry. I can take care of myself." He doesn't reply and instead just gives me one last look before walking into his office.

I take a deep breath. I need to stop lusting after him, but he is making it bloody difficult.

Chapter 3

Tommy

My hand hovers over the door handle to Ella's office. *Fucking Ian again!* The voice and accent of my head chef are easy to identify. This is the third time this week that he is hanging out with my assistant. Even if I have no right to be jealous I can feel it deep in my guts. Trying to get control over myself, I take a deep breath and push the door to the office open.

"Ian, you're spending more time in my office nowadays than in the kitchen. Want to apply for an admin position?" My voice drips with sarcasm and Ian gives me a glare.

"Funny, Tommy," he says but there is no laughter. "I came to see if you want me in the meeting with the people from the VIP fundraiser." If Ian likes anything more than running after the female staff it's putting his face front and centre. I would have fired him a long time ago, but Anna keeps reminding me that disliking his attitude is not enough and there are employment laws to follow. Unfortunately, the female staff members never make an official complaint, I have yet to catch him in the act, and the guests love his food, so the feedback is first class. If I fired him now I would be in front of an employment tribunal in a heartbeat.

We managed to give him two warnings based on hearsay only, so Anna insists we need a proper reason for the final warning before we can dismiss him.

"That's fine, Ian, thank you. I've got it." I cross my arms over my chest. Ian is no taller than five foot eight and so I tower over him at six foot four inches.

"What if they have questions about the food?"

"Then I'll answer them," I reply firmly. My eyes drift briefly to Ella and I can see her biting her lips to hold in a laugh. "Ian, I've run this hotel for over ten years, I think I can handle a simple meeting." I know he hates to be called Ian, but I won't stand for this chef nonsense.

"Fine, it was just an offer. I'll see you later, love," he says looking at Ella and ignoring me. *What a prick.*

"Her name is Ella." My tone is cold. "She is your colleague and I expect you to show her the respect she deserves." Ian's face is turning red, but he doesn't reply. Instead, he just walks past me and leaves the office.

"What did he want?" My question sounds harsh.

"What he said. You interrupted before he could ask me out again." She looks at me with big eyes and I have to remind myself to breathe.

"You two are dating," I growl.

"God, no. No, no, no. I would rather run naked through Fellside," she exclaims and her cheeks turn pink. The image of her naked body flashes through my mind and I know I need to get out of here. *Fuck!* I slide my fingers through my hair just as the phone on Ella's desk starts to ring.

17

"Thanks, Tommy will be down in a minute. Can you please put them in the Oak Room?" she tells the person on the other end. The Oak Room is our ornate fine dining restaurant, and I prefer to conduct important meetings there when I want to make a strong impression.

"Virginia from the Rotary Club is here," Ella explains after she puts the phone down. I just nod. My mind is not really in the game today, and having to schmooze these people and convince them to hold their big fundraising gala in our hotel is the last thing I want to do. But I also know that this event is worth a lot of money and we need it to help finance the extension I am planning to add to the hotel.

We have a lot of large events but not enough bedrooms to put up all the guests and so adding twenty new rooms to the hotel is a no-brainer. I am meeting with some architecture firms next week to look at their plans before we decide on one and I can't wait. I have some vivid ideas for the extension which is why the tender document was thirty pages long. I wasn't sure if I should send it but Ella convinced me that there would be no point in holding back when I feel so strongly about what I want. I'd only set myself up for disappointment.

"Thanks, do you have the brochure for me please?" I try to give her a smile. *Don't be a grump, don't be a grump.*

"Here." She grabs the cream-coloured folder from her desk and stands up. Now I can see that she is wearing black trousers today rather than a pencil skirt and I almost comment on them until I realise it would be inappropriate.

Ella hands me the folder and softly says, "Wait." She reaches out and gently pushes my tie into place before pulling it tight. She is so close that I can feel her warmth and take in her scent. Our eyes are locked and I can feel my dick getting hard. *Jeez.*

That's the last thing I need in the business meeting, a boner.

"Thanks," I say again but now my voice sounds strained. I take a step back before turning and leaving the office. This woman is going to be the death of me.

* * *

"It was a pleasure to meet you, Virginia." I shake her hand before Sheila, my Operations Manager, escorts her to the exit.

"How was the meeting?" I turn to see Ella standing at the foot of the oak staircase.

"I think we'll get the business," I grin. She gives me a big smile in return.

"That's amazing! That will be so helpful when talking to the bank for the loan." I love that she is as enthusiastic about my hotel as I am. I have met many phony people in my life and I know when someone is just blowing smoke up my arse.

"I know..., Ella, you have—" I point towards the dark spec in the corner of her mouth.

"What?" She wipes over her lips but misses what I suspect to be chocolate traces. She nibbles on that stuff all day long. I take a step closer and wipe with my thumb the crumbs away. Her breath catches when I make contact with her skin.

"There," I say before sucking the chocolate from my thumb. My breathing is faster and I am lost in her eyes. Ella just looks at me with a blush covering her cheeks.

"Tommy, there you are." A woman's voice makes Ella turn her head and break our eye contact. I feel like I have been ripped out of my happy place back into cold reality.

"Hi, Tommy," a second woman says and my eyes finally drift away from Ella and what I see causes me to panic. *Alex is going to be a dead man.*

"Christina, Emma... and Charlotte, what are you doing here?" I ask with dread in my voice.

"Well, Phil's sister is looking after Lilly; Jane loves to play the doting aunt. That means mum," she points at herself, "has the day off and so I convinced these two beauties to have a ladies' lunch. And where better than your hotel," Christina explains with way too much enthusiasm and I notice that her eyes keep darting to Ella. Emma and Charlotte, who both stand behind Christina look at me innocently but the blush on Emma's cheeks tells me there is much more behind this visit.

"You must be Ella," Christina introduces herself to my assistant. "We have heard so much about you." Yup, Alex or Nick or both definitely opened their big mouths because I have never mentioned Ella before to anyone else in the group.

Ella looks at me with a shell shocked expression and I just shrug. I'm not sure what else to do.

"Ella, these are Christina, Charlotte and Emma. They are the partners of some of my FMR mates." I point out my friends to her.

"It's nice to meet you," Ella says politely and she is greeted by three big, knowing smiles. They are definitely here to meddle.

"Are you from around here?" Charlotte finally speaks up.

"No, I'm originally from Manchester, but I moved here when I got the job with Tommy."

"And I bet our workaholic won't let you have time off to make friends," Christina laughs and slaps me playfully on the chest before linking her arm with Ella's. "You must have lunch with us. You don't mind, Tommy, do you?" She grins. Panic rises in me again. Christina has no filter, and I can't be sure what she will tell Ella, but what reason could I give for Ella not to take a lunch break?

"I... sure, no, that's fine if Ella wants to."

"Sure she does," Christina answers for her.

Ella laughs. "Apparently, I do. To be honest, Chef has a new pie on the menu that I have been dying to try."

"See!" Christina gives me a triumphant grin.

"Ella, please put the lunch on my tab," I offer.

"Oh, you don't have to," Emma tries to interject. She is clearly uncomfortable.

"Thanks, Tommy," Christina giggles at the same time. "Let's go," she commands and drags Ella off towards the restaurant with Charlotte hot on her heels. *Yes, run but you can't hide.* I gently grab Emma's arm before she can follow them.

"What did Alex tell you?" My voice sounds cold and I am sure I have a deep frown on my face.

"He..., I am sorry, Tommy. He told me what you said at the rescue and I mentioned it to Christina, and you know her."

"Yes, I do. You need to make sure she keeps this to herself, Emma. Please!"

"I'll try. I'm really sorry."

"I know." I give her a hug. Emma would never hurt anyone and I didn't mean to upset her. It's Christina I don't trust because she has a habit of putting her foot in it and blurting out things she shouldn't.

"We just want you to be happy, Tommy." she sniffles.

"I am happy," I declare trying to sound convincing but even I can hear that there isn't real conviction behind the words. "Now go and make sure Christina behaves," I usher her towards the restaurant.

I watch her walk down the long corridor. *Fuck!* I ruffle my hair again before pulling my phone from my pocket.

Me: I can't believe you told Emma.

The reply is immediate.

Alex: She's my wife.
Me: She told Christina.
Alex: Oh shit.
Me: They are here to have lunch and Christina invited Ella to join them.
Alex: You are fucked, man.

Yes, yes that I am.

Chapter 4

Ella

I can't remember the last time I laughed so much. Christina has been telling me all about how she pursued Phil, or Bambi, as she loves to call him. She hinted that both Emma and Charlotte had similar interesting stories on how they met their significant others but she left it at that.

I felt an immediate connection to all three of them. They are just the kind of people you want to have as friends.

"So, what about you?" Charlotte asks before putting a spoon full of spotted dick in her mouth.

"I'm single," I say but involuntarily add a sigh to it.

"Ah, but you don't want to be," Christina picks me up on it.

"Well, I wouldn't say no if the right person came along." Warmth rises in my cheeks. Of course, an image of Tommy in his FMR outfit pops into my head. I love the look of him in his mountaineering gear.

"The right person like a certain hotel owner?" she asks with a smirk on her face.

"No!" I almost shout but I also feel that my cheeks are full at blaze now.

"I know that blush," Emma grins at me.

"No, he is my boss," I whisper. Our staff are nosy and the last thing I need is for rumours to spread through the hotel.

"So? You wouldn't be the first two people who work together that fall for each other," Charlotte says and I appreciate that she keeps the conversation also to a whisper.

"Tommy is not falling for me."

"Ahem, did we not walk in on the two of you, mooning over each other with him wiping your lip and then sucking his thumb? Please! If Phil had done that when we started dating, I would have creamed my knickers."

"Christina!" Emma gives her friend a stern look.

"What? It's true," Christina laughs.

My heart starts beating faster. She's right. There was something so intimate about our interaction earlier, I nearly moaned when he slid his thumb over my mouth. But could he really be interested in me?

"He has been nothing but grumpy around me," I reply.

"Since when is Tommy grumpy?" Charlotte asks but then her eyes light up in excitement. "Or maybe he is grumpy to keep you at a distance because he thinks you are not interested and he's your boss. He's way too much of a good guy to abuse his position," she adds with glee and Emma and Christina nod in agreement. They jumped to that conclusion too quick. Did he talk about me?

"No way. I don't think so." I sound weak and my doubt of my own words is apparent.

"Ella, you're right, we don't know," Emma says. She stops Christina, who wants to interrupt, with another stern look. "But just consider the possibility. If you like him, watch out for signs and if you see them and the opportunity presents itself, don't let him slip away. He is a good guy and there aren't many like him. Trust me. I know."

Her words hit home. Did I interpret his grumpiness wrong? What if it isn't that he doesn't like me. What if it is the opposite. I take a deep breath and finally nod.

"Yeah," Christina cheers as if we won the grand prize in the lottery. "And you can test our theory tonight. Come to the pub with us. We are all meeting for our monthly get together, and Tommy will be there."

"I have to check if he is okay with it. I'd be invading his personal life."

"Pish-posh. I have invited you. That has nothing to do with Tommy," she interjects.

"I'll ask him," I reply firmly before waving the waitress over to get the bill ready so I can sign it for accounts.

After I've said goodbye to the ladies I walk back to my office. I carefully balance my tablet and a plate of food for Tommy whilst trying to open the door. Eventually I manage to push it open without spilling any gravy.

"Ella?" Tommy calls out the minute I walk through the door.

"I brought lunch," I reply. I place my tablet on the desk and then walk into Tommy's office. His door is open as usual. "Here you go." I place the plate with the roast chicken on his desk.

"A waitress could have done that," he says, his voice deep and growly.

"Sure, but I was coming this way anyway." I shrug and walk back towards the door.

"How was lunch?" Do I hear concern in his voice? I stop my walk and look back at him.

"It was lovely. They are a lot of fun. In fact, they invited me to the pub tonight," I add. Tommy's eyes widen for a second.

"If that's okay with you?" I ask cautiously.

"Sure..., why wouldn't it be?" he asks but there is an edge to his voice.

"Well, I don't want you to think I'm invading your personal life." Our eyes are locked and there is an electric tension in the air.

"You should come," he says finally. "I can give you a lift if you want."

"Oh, that would be great, thanks." I don't drive and I was planning to walk but if I can save myself the twenty-minute hike, I won't say no to that.

"Great."

"Great," I agree before turning and walking back to my desk. There are about a thousand knots in my stomach. Or are they butterflies? I can't be sure.

* * *

"Sorry we're late," a tall, dark and handsome guy says as he and his partner drop into chairs opposite me. Honestly, not sure what the entry requirements are for FMR but being hot must be one of them. I look around the table and every guy is handsome in their own way.

"Ella, this is Chris and his wife Suzie. They are the remaining members of our FMR unit. Now you've met them all," Tommy introduces me. He hasn't left my side since we arrived and shooed Christina away when she tried to take his seat next to me. This of course made her give me a knowing smile.

"Well, I am on a bit of a break from FMR," Suzie laughs and rubs her baby bump. Chris kisses her softly before placing

26

a protective hand on her round tummy. Could they be more swoon-worthy?

"It's nice to meet you, Ella." Chris smiles at me.

"So why are you late?" Rob asks from the other end of the table. "We thought you wouldn't come at all."

"Mate, drama with Max."

"Max is our son," Suzie explains for my benefit. "And we now have a snail as a pet."

"Excuse me?" Alex asks.

"Snail Bail." Chris looks a little sheepish.

"Snail Bail?" Alex laughs so hard that everyone else starts laughing as well.

"And what, he was moving too slow back into the stable, is that why you're late?" Nick mimics the slow pace of a snail wiggling along on the table and everyone bursts out laughing again.

"No, me and Max were arguing that snails are not pets," Suzie explains, "There were tears and then this one," she points at her husband, "can't say no to him and now we have a snail in an old fish tank in the kitchen."

"Max was so happy." Chris just shrugs and grins. He clearly isn't sorry that he's given in. Everyone else bursts out laughing again.

I lean back in my chair and take everything in. They have the kind of friendship I have never had in my life. It feels more like a family than just friends. I almost envy Tommy for them, but then, they have somehow accepted me into the group and are treating me like one of their own, so maybe I don't need to be envious.

Tommy is different around them. He is relaxed and less serious. I have never seen him laugh this much. A while ago he

27

placed his arm on the back of my chair and it has stayed there ever since. He doesn't really have his arm around me because he is barely touching me, but it still has set off a thousand butterflies in my tummy.

"Are you okay," he suddenly whispers in my ear. His warm breath blows gently over my neck and goosebumps form on my arms. I turn my head and look at him.

"Sure, why do you ask?"

"You looked lost in thought."

"I was just thinking how lucky you are to have such amazing friends," I say truthfully.

"They are my family. But I think they've adopted you as well. You are one of us now," he chuckles.

"Are you okay with that?" I am terrified he might think I am overstepping a line. His eyes are lock on mine and he takes a deep breath.

"Absolutely." It is just one word but there is more to this, I can feel it. Tommy turns to Nick who is sitting next to him and I let out a slow breath. When I look around the table, Christina smiles at me and gives me a wink. Of course she saw that.

* * *

"So did you have fun?" Tommy asks as he indicates to turn left. He insisted on driving me home even if it is only a short walk to my flat.

"So much fun! They are all hilarious."

"They liked you," he replies with his eyes fixed on the road.

"Well, I gave them all the gossip about you," I giggle and poke him in the shoulder. Tommy laughs out loud. It has been great to see him laugh and smile all evening. Jeez, if I thought the grumpy man was hot, a happy and cheerful Tommy definitely made me, to quote Christina, cream my knickers.

"It's just over there, the small block of flats." I point to the left at the grey building. Tommy slides the car into a parking spot and turns off the engine.

"Ella, I think I need to apologise." He turns in his seat and looks at me.

"What for?"

"For being a moody arsehole since you started." He leans his head against the seat, but his eyes are still locked on mine.

"Well, I wouldn't quite put it like this, but I did nickname you Lord Grumpiness," I giggle.

Tommy doesn't laugh. Instead, he reaches out and pushes a strand of hair behind my ear.

"I'm sorry."

"Why were you so grumpy to me?" I hold my breath waiting for his answer.

"I... I like you."

"And that's why you were grumpy?" I need him to say what I think he means to say. Absent-mindedly, he taps on the steering wheel and stares into the darkness through the windscreen.

"I like you, Ella. I like you a lot, but I am your boss and in order to keep my distance, I—" I stop him by gently cupping his face, turning it to me and pressing my lips to his. The minute we connect, he takes over. He slides his hands into my hair and turns my head to deepen the kiss. His tongue slowly strokes over my lip until I open up for him. I never thought a kiss could feel as loaded and intense as this kiss does. After what feels like an eternity and in equal measure like a fraction of a second, I move away from him. I need to get out of the car before I ask him to fuck me in the middle of the car park. I want him, he wants me, but it's not that easy. We work together. I need to get a clear head and think about this. I have fancied him for months now, but I never thought past the point of what would happen if we got together because it felt so impossible.

"Good night," I say before leaving his car and walking towards the building. Tommy waits until I open the door and only then starts his engine and pulls out onto the road. I don't dare to turn around, even if all I want to do is have a last glimpse of him.

Chapter 5

Tommy

Nervously, I straighten my tie for the fifth time. It has been two days since Ella and I kissed and I still don't know how I'll handle it when I'll have to face her in a bit. Whilst weekends don't really exist for me, Ella is off every Saturday and Sunday, so I haven't seen her since that kiss.

More than once over the last two days I have typed out a text message and every single one of them sounded stupid, so I deleted it again.

"Fuck!" I swear loudly before grabbing my rucksack and garment bag. Not only do I need to face Ella today, but we are also travelling to Manchester together to meet with different architecture companies for the expansion project. And we are staying overnight in the hotel of a friend of mine. The thought of spending so much time together makes my dick twitch with excitement and my stomach knot up with nerves.

"Morning, boss," John, our apprentice on reception, says when I walk past the desk. He grabs my keys and luggage and carries them outside to my car. He is a good lad and he takes on even the most menial tasks with an enthusiasm that is rare in today's youth.

"Thanks, John," I call after him before turning to the receptionist. "Sheila is in charge, but if there are any issues you can call me or Ella," I tell the young receptionist whose name I have forgotten. She has only been with us for a few weeks and with more than fifty staff working for me I tend to only learn people's names once I know they are really staying.

As I walk into the sunshine, I can see Ella leaning against my BMW X5. It is one of the few expensive things I have ever splashed out for in my life, but when I needed a new car I gave the Range Rover, which is so popular around here, a miss and opted for a bit more luxury.

"Hi." She gives me a small smile and nibbles on her bottom lip.

"Hey," I reply. I am glad that I am not the only one who is nervous. I briefly glance at my watch before accepting my car key back from John.

"You're in charge, John." I wink at him and he chuckles. He reminds me a lot of myself at his age and I can see him staying in the sector. He has the right mentality for it.

"We should go, there are some roadworks between here and Windermere," I comment before climbing into the car. I throw my jacket on the backseat and put the seatbelt on. Ella joins me and buckles up in the passenger seat.

Neither of us says anything as I pull out of the parking spot. A soft strand of her hair slides over my hand as I place it on the back of her chair when looking behind me to reverse. Immediately the image from Friday night is conjured up when I grabbed hold of her hair whilst kissing her. Ella is staring straight ahead and is not moving. Guilt hits me. I definitely made a mistake kissing her. She is uncomfortable now and it is my fault. *I can't lose her.* Not just because she is an amazing assistant but also because I rather have her in my life as just a friend than not at all.

After another five minutes of silence, I can't take it anymore. "Ella—"

"I'm sorry, Tommy!" she blurts out before I can finish my sentence. I glance at her as we drive along Lake Windermere. Fellside sits on one end of the lake and the town of Windermere at the other.

"What are you sorry for?"

"For attacking you in your car," she whispers and puts her head in her hands. I laugh out loud. I can't stop it.

"Well, I'm glad you find my embarrassment so funny," Ella says angrily. I indicate and turn the car into one of the many lay-bys tourists use to take photos of the lake.

"What are you doing?" she asks.

"Stopping so I don't cause an accident." I turn off the engine, unfasten my seatbelt and turn in my seat to face her.

"Ella, look at me." It sounds like an order and so I add, "Please?" She continues to avoid eye contact, so, I reach out and turn her face to mine. "Ella, what gave you the impression that I didn't like what happened on Friday night?" She pulls her bottom lip between her teeth again to nibble on it nervously. "I think it was my tongue in your mouth and not the other way round," I chuckle. A small smile flickers over her face and her eyes darken.

"Oh, Ella." I cup her face. " You've been driving me crazy ever since you started working at Greenview. But I am your boss. I didn't want you to feel uncomfortable so I would have never made the first move."

"And then I did."

33

"And then you did. Now I am not sure what to do. I don't want to go back to how it was before."

"Me neither. But you are still my boss."

"I know." I lean back against my seat and let go of her. "Let's get the next two days over with and then discuss how we handle this when we are back at Fellside. How does that sound?"

"Sounds like a plan," she agrees but I can see on her face that she is a little disappointed. "So, just to clarify, no kissing?"

"That depends."

"On what?"

"On you. Again, I don't want to make you uncomfortable." I look at her. I want to do the right thing, but I can't deny how much I want her.

"So, hypothetically, if we wanted to see if we are even compat-ible," she pretends to think very hard, "we could have a repeat of Friday night?"

"Hypothetically," I agree with a grin.

"Maybe even more."

"Maybe."

"I mean, we might just not gel. You might be terrible in bed," she giggles.

"Excuse me?" I mock indignation.

"I have very high standards." She twirls a strand of hair around her finger. "I mean, the kiss was promising but..." She leaves the rest of the sentence hang in the air. I laugh out loud.

"So, you want to use the next two days to see if we fit?" I ask more seriously. I need to hear it straight out.

"Yes."

"And what if it's a disaster?"

"Then we return to Fellside and pretend it never happened," she shrugs. If only it were that easy, but my need for her overrides all of my concerns.

"What happens in Manchester, stays in Manchester?"

"Exactly," she giggles.

"Okay," I finally agree, and Ella relaxes in her seat. My finger is about to push the start button for the car when I stop myself. My hand slides around Ella's neck and pulls her closer. When my lips meet hers, I relax for the first time since Friday. Kissing her feels like coming home after a long journey. Ella moans and I deepen the kiss. When my tongue slides over hers I groan. Nothing has ever felt so good. I take a last lick before breaking away.

"And just so you know, Ella, when I finally get you into bed, it will be fantastic." She locks eyes with me and laughs.

"Cocky much? Are you that good?"

"No, but the two of us together will be perfect." There is no humour in my voice and Ella's eyes widen.

I finally start the car and pull out of the lay-by.

Chapter 6

Ella

"Mr Hunter, it is a pleasure to welcome you to the Whitworth Townhouse Hotel," the young concierge greets us as we step into the lobby. The term *townhouse* in the hotel name is grossly misleading. It makes it sound quaint and small when it is everything but. Yes, it is made up of a number of old Georgian townhouses but that is really the only connection to that word. It is a grand and luxurious five-star hotel in the centre of Manchester. The fact that they have a concierge says everything, as this is definitely a job title on the way to becoming extinct.

I feel him glance at me. He must know that we have two rooms booked, but Tommy's hand on my lower back doesn't scream employer-employee relationship.

"Thank you, this is Ms Grange," Tommy introduces me. The concierge smiles politely, even if Tommy has failed to clarify who I really am.

"I hope you will enjoy your stay with us, Ms Grange." He ushers us to the check in desk and after we have signed our registration form, we are escorted to two junior suites on the top floor of the building. We did of course book normal rooms; Tommy doesn't like wasting money and we're only here for one day. But his friend, who owns this place, insisted on upgrading us.

Before we retire to our own rooms, we agree to meet for dinner in an hour, which should give me just enough time to wash the day off and get ready.

Tommy and I spent all afternoon with two architecture firms who have put forward a tender for the hotel extensions. The designs were not bad, but I could see on Tommy's face that he wasn't particularly taken by either. Deep in my guts I know he will choose my family's design. Not because they are my family, Tommy is way too professional for that. No, he will love the design. I know what is important to him in the hotel and I made sure it's all integrated in the design. A wave of guilt hits me again. I should tell him the truth.

My phone rings and I see Lee's name on the display. Perfect timing. It is like he can feel me fighting my conscience. I could ignore him but he will just keep calling until I answer. With a shaking hand I pick it up.

"Hi, Lee."

"How did it go to today," he barks down the phone.

"I can't—"

"Ella, don't fuck with me. You know how important this is for the business. If we don't get this contract we are done for. So, tell me. Did he like any of them?" Despite the firm having had many successes in the past, Lee and my dad are not good with money. They also lost a number of significant contracts after I left and Lee had to take care of the creative side of the company. Snagging the contract for Tommy's extension would really help them out financially.

I sit down on my bed and try to calm my breathing.

"He didn't like them."

"Are you sure?"

"Yes. They were not bad designs but very modern. It wouldn't fit in with Greenview Manor's concept."

"Good. I want you to work on him tonight."

"What?"

"Convince him we are the best option."

"Lee, he knows it's my family. He will tell me it's a conflict of interest."

"Ella, don't be stupid. Do it in a subtle way. I'll see you tomorrow." He hangs up before I can reply. *I won't do it. No, I won't do it!* I am shaking with anger, and frustration and fear. *No, I won't do it.*

* * *

I sigh when I look at myself in the mirror. In my naivety, thinking we would ignore Friday and act all professional, I only brought a business outfit for tomorrow and a casual jeans and T-shirt combo for the evening. And that's all I have to wear now. There is nothing seductive or sexy on it.

A knock on the door stops me from wishing for a miracle Cinderella-like transformation. I grab my simple black handbag and open the door.

Give me strength, how does he look so effortlessly hot? He is also just wearing jeans and a simple long-sleeved T-shirt but, in his case, he looks like a sportswear model. His T-shirt clings to his body and I can see the outlines of his muscles. *Am I drooling? It feels like I'm drooling.*

"Hey," he greets me and places a soft kiss on my cheek. He smells fresh and clean with a hint of aftershave. Just breathing in his scent makes my pussy tingle.

"Hi, sorry, we may have to go somewhere casual for dinner. I didn't think of bringing anything fancy." I can feel heat in my cheeks. Tommy's eyes move up and down my body.

"You look perfect in anything." *Oh boy.* He helps me into my jacket and then slides his hand in mine and links our fingers.

"Come on."

"Where are we going?"

"The most exclusive place in Manchester," he replies with a wink.

"Tommy, I told you—" I pull him to a halt.

"Ella, trust me, you are perfectly dressed for where I'm taking you." He pulls me along the corridor but bypasses the lift and pushes the door open to the stairs.

"Is the lift broken?" I really don't fancy fourteen floors of stairs, even if it is descending them.

"Nope," he chuckles as we step into the staircase. "We're going up and there is no lift." We climb a few stairs until we reach a door with a sign warning that access is for staff only. Tommy pulls the door open and we step outside into the cool air. I freeze at the spot. We are on the roof of the hotel. In one corner there are air vents and air conditioning units, but at the other end, with a view overlooking Manchester, is a small table under a pergola covered in fairy lights. There are outdoor pyramid heaters placed around it to give some warmth and their flames add to the romantic setting.

"This is amazing," I whisper.

"It is, isn't it?" Tommy smiles. "I can't take credit. Nick proposed to Charlotte up here and asked the hotel to set this

39

up for that moment. Well, slightly less elaborately. The hotel's marketing team loved the idea and they have kept it and offer it as an exclusive dining experience to VIP guests."

"We are VIPs?" I smirk.

"No, but I have friends in high places," Tommy chuckles and pulls me to the pergola. "I know it's chilly today, but I thought we could at least try it and if it gets too cold, we can move the dinner to one of our rooms." He shrugs and insecurity flashes over his face.

"It's perfect," I say and yank him to me before placing a soft kiss on his mouth. His hand slides around my waist to align our bodies.

"Ella—" he sighs. "Let's eat." I am sure that's not what he wanted to say but I'll let it go.

The food is as amazing as is the setting and the view. By the time they bring a fancy version of Eton Mess, I am not sure if I can take another bite. Tommy has been relaxed and flirty all evening. He doesn't seem to be able to stop touching me and I don't want him to.

We share the dessert. There has been a spark in the air all night, but nothing compared to when he feeds me the sweet meringue. If the waiter hadn't interrupted us, I think Tommy would have pulled me into his lap then and there.

The staff quickly clear our food away before discreetly disappearing again. I give him what I hope to be a seductive smile before walking to the railing surrounding the hotel roof and looking down at the blinking lights of Manchester.

"What are you thinking?" Tommy steps up next to me.

"This has been an amazing evening," I reply as I place my hands on the railing. Tommy takes a few steps, slides his hands around my waist from behind me and pulls me close. My back collides with his chest. He places his chin on my shoulder.

"Now it's perfect," he whispers.

I don't reply. I just melt into his embrace. His warmth seeps into me and I wish I could stop time. In this moment all my problems seem so far away: Lee, the fact that Tommy is my boss, Lee... No, I don't want to think about this.

"Not quite perfect," I finally say into the night air.

"What would make it perfect?"

I swipe my hair to the side to expose my neck. "Your lips right here." I point at the sensitive spot under my ear. I have dreamed about him kissing me there.

Tommy chuckles and leans forward. However, he doesn't give me what I want, at least not right away. He places soft kisses where my collar bone ends and my neck starts and then ever so slowly slides his lips up. His stubble scratches softly over my sensitive skin and the tender touch makes my clit tingle. When he finally licks over the spot I showed him, I moan.

"Tommy, I need more," I sigh and push his hands from my hips towards my pussy. I have been waiting for this for months. In this moment I don't care that the waiters could return any minute. I have lost all sense of reality.

Tommy lifts one of his hands and uses it to grab by chin and turn my head. He captures my lips in a searing kiss whilst his other hand pulls my zip open and slides inside my trousers. His hand is cold from the night air and causes me to shiver when it makes the first contact with my skin.

"More," I mumble. And he finally gives me what I want. His thumb swipes over my clit and two fingers dip into my pussy. He is not tender or building my arousal slowly. He must also be aware that we could get discovered any minute.

"Fuck," I hiss as he finger-fucks me. I press my arse into him and I can feel his hard cock. Of course, I assumed that this would arouse him as well but to feel the evidence so clearly pushes me over the edge. I scream his name and it echoes over the roof tops of Manchester.

"Oh shit," I whisper as if I could take the scream back and place my hand over my mouth. Tommy chuckles and pulls his hand from my jeans. I turn just as he licks two of his fingers clean. I scrunch up my face.

"What?" he asks.

"You could have just wiped that on—" I am not sure what on.

"Are you mad? I have been dying to taste you. And you taste amazing," he replies with his eyes dark and hooded by desire. "Try." He holds out his thumb.

"Eew, no!" I slap him gently on his chest. He shrugs, licks his thumb clean as well before pulling me into a kiss. *Bastard.* I can taste myself on his tongue and I have to admit it actually arouses me. But over my dead body would I tell him that.

"See," he smirks when a noticeable shiver rushes through me.

"Tommy, take me to your room," I reply. That wipes the smirk of his face.

"Are you sure?"

"I have never been more sure of anything."

Chapter 7

Tommy

T he minute the door closes behind us, I press Ella against it. Our eyes lock with a fiery intensity, and I can feel the desire burning between us. We are drawn to each other, unable to resist the strong attraction. I cup her face and our lips meet in a passionate, electric kiss. Our hands find each other, and we explore each other's bodies with urgency, wanting to be as close as possible. Time seems to vanish as we lose ourselves in the intensity of that kiss. It's a moment filled with raw passion, and I know it will leave a lasting mark on my heart.

Then Ella softly pushes me back and steps from my embrace. She gives me a shy look over her shoulder as she walks towards the bed before lifting her T-shirt over her head and dropping it on the floor. As she reaches the bed, she turns and locks eyes with me. I hear the zip of her jeans as she slides it down. She slowly pushes her trousers over her hips and steps out of them.

I swallow hard when I take in her perfect beauty. She is standing there with a cautious smile on her face wearing nothing more than green lacy knickers and a bra.

I rush to her, ripping my own T-shirt over my head, and throwing it behind me. The second I reach her I pull her back into my arms and melt into another kiss with her. Her fingers slide over my chest and, fuck, do I need her.

I lift her and gently throw her onto the mattress. She giggles, but the giggles turn into a moan the minute my lips land on her neck. I kiss my way downwards whilst my fingers push the cup of her bra aside. My thumb strokes over one of her nipples before I catch it between my lips and softly suck on it.

"Tommy," she whispers and her hands find their way into my hair.

"Tell me what you need, babe."

"I need you to fuck me," she moans and tries to rub her lace covered pussy against my crotch. Instinct takes over and I push my hard dick against her.

"No, naked, you need to be naked," she says through hard breathing. *Fuck!* I am basically dry humping her. I move from the bed and strip of the rest of my clothes. When my eyes land on her as she wriggles in need on the bed, I absent-mindedly grab my cock and pump it one, two times.

"Tommy!" She holds out her hand and waves me back to her. I step up to the bed, hook my fingers into the each side of her knickers and pull them down. I am about to crawl over her when I suddenly remember.

"Shit," I swear loudly and Ella's eyes widen in surprise. "Condom," I explain and walk over to my bag. Fine, yes, I brought some with me, just in case.

"You have a mighty fine arse, Mr Hunter," she giggles. I look over my shoulder and see her sitting on the bed. I grin and playfully shake my backside. Ella throws her head back and laughs out loud.

I grab the foil packet, rip it open and roll on the condom as I walk back to her. I bend forward and kiss her deeply.

"How do you want it, baby?"

"I don't care as long as I can look into your eyes," she sighs as she touches her forehead against mine. I scoop her up and place her into the centre of the bed before leaning over her. I align myself and push into her warm pussy. *So, this is what perfection feels like.* I groan deeply and hold myself above her. I want to make this last as long as I can, but Ella doesn't agree with that.

She places both of her feet on the mattress and lifts her hips up to meet me head on. I take a deep breath and match her rhythm. I pump into her and her pussy squeezes me hard every time I pull out.

"Fuck, Ella, I won't last this way, you need to slow down," I say through clenched teeth.

"No fucking way, don't hold back, please, I need this. I waited so long for it." *Shit*, her admission that she has also wanted me for much longer than just the kiss on Friday makes me lose all control and I push into her hard and fast. I can feel the tightening at the base of my spine.

"I touched myself so often picturing you doing this," she whispers with her eyes locked on me. She slides her hand between us and starts to circle her clit. "Like this."

That's too much for me. I hammer into her, my eyes always on her. Just when I feel I can't hold any longer, she calls out my name and I follow her with my own orgasm.

I am paralysed for a few minutes with my head in the crook of her neck. I can feel her warmth under me, her smell engulfs me and my mouth remembers her sweet taste. Then I realise that my whole weight is on her.

"Fuck, sorry, baby." I push up on my arms and look down on

45

her.

"What's a better word than perfect? I really feel perfect is not enough for what just happened," she smiles at me and gently strokes my sweat-soaked hair from my face.

I give her a soft kiss and then roll off her. I dispose of the condom in the bathroom bin and grab a towel. I wet it under the tap with warm water and return to the bedroom. Ella hasn't moved. The only indication that she hasn't fallen asleep on me is that she is playing with a strand of her hair. I switch off the light and walk back to the bed in the dim light filtering through the curtains.

"Open your legs, baby," I whisper softly and I wipe her with the towel before throwing it through the open bathroom door.

We crawl under the duvet and I cuddle up behind her. She pulls the arm I have draped over her waist higher and snuggles her face into my palm.

"Can we stay here forever?" she asks into the darkness.

"Imagine all the brilliant things we'll miss."

"Like what? This feels pretty great to me."

"It is, for the lack of a better word, perfect," I chuckle. "But I would like to do so many things with you. I want to show you my favourite spot in the hills. I want to take you for éclairs at Cherry Pie, I want to cook my favourite food for you, I want to have an argument with you so we can make up like bunnies." My last comment makes her laugh out loud.

"Or bungee jumping?"

"You want to bungee jump?" I ask.

"Maybe, although I'm scared of heights."

"I'll take you bungee jumping, if that's what you want."

"You are too busy for all of that, Tommy," she giggles, but immediately a heaviness descends on this conversation.

46

"I would make time for you." And I mean it. The thought of sharing life with her, not just this stolen moment, makes me feel a deep happiness.

"Are you sure about that?"

"To be honest, I wonder if my long hours are down to me having nothing else in my life. Well, except for the guys and FMR, but hanging out with them lately has been difficult because it reminds me that it is just me. It has been just me since my parents died."

"No other woman? I heard rumours of a she-monster or something."

"She-devil. No, she was when my parents were still alive."

"Want to tell me about her?" She softly strokes over my arm.

"Not much to tell. I thought I was in love with her. My dad warned me that something didn't seem right. Turned out that she was after the hotel. She thought if she married me she would be the boss. But that's not how things work. She quickly found out that me having the hotel meant a lot of debt and not a lot of money to splash around. She dumped me after I told her to stop using the staff as personal slaves." I pull Ella closer and take a deep breath to draw her scent in. It's driving me crazy.

"I'm sorry, Tommy, it must have been hard to lose someone you loved like that."

"I didn't love her. I realised that afterwards. I loved the feeling of being with her. But when she walked out of my life, I didn't miss her. I was actually glad she was gone."

"And then you started to call her *she-devil*?" Ella laughs.

"Nope, it was Alex who came up with that. She tried to get me to drop FMR and he lost it. Even if I would have never done it. I promised my dad."

"I'm glad you didn't give up FMR. It gets you out of the hotel once in a while."

I laugh. She's right, it does.

"What about you?"

"What about me?"

"You know everything about my life, and I know hardly anything."

"Firstly, I don't know everything. And secondly, Lord Grumpiness, whose fault is it that we haven't had a single non-work-related conversation until a couple of days ago?" I pinch her gently in her side and she squeals. She's right though.

"It was safer."

"Safer?"

"Fuck, Ella, the minute you walked through my door I was a goner."

"Yeah, you're right, being grumpy in that case makes total sense," she muses.

"It did. I didn't think it was appropriate for me to drool over you."

"What about now?"

"We'll make it work, if you want to give us a chance." Ella turns in my arms and cups my face.

"I don't want to be anywhere other than with you. We can't help who we fall for and nothing inappropriate has happened."

"Not sure everyone will see it that way and I am willing to die on that hill. But you know it is always the woman that gets blamed. It's ridiculous, but—"

"People will always talk, Tommy. Especially in Fellside. But we know and our friends know the truth ." I place a soft kiss on her mouth.

"Now we are talking about me again! Tell me something about you." Ella shifts to turn her back to me again.

"What do you want to know?"

"Why Fellside?"

"Manchester was just not for me. I felt trapped here. There was no place for me in my family's business and I hate city life. When I came to Fellside for a break, I fell in love with the village and I knew I had to live there. Then I saw Greenview Manor and what you created there is amazing."

"I can't take all the credit. Mr Sinder started it all."

"But you gave it the soul that people love so much."

"Maybe. What about your friends, lovers?" I try to bring the attention back to her.

"I didn't have many friends in Manchester. My last relationship ended two years ago. It just fizzled out. No drama. I am not trying to be cryptic, Tommy, but there really wasn't much in my life before I came to Fellside. This is the first time I've felt at home somewhere," she sighs. Despite her reassurance, I have a feeling there is a lot more to say about this but she snuggles back into me.

"I think we should sleep; we have three presentations to listen to tomorrow." Ella ends our conversation. She turns her head for a final kiss and, as I pull her closer, I promise myself that I will do everything to make this work.

Chapter 8

Ella

I drop another sugar cube in my black coffee and try to stifle a yawn. We are in meeting two of three and I am struggling. Tommy woke me up at six with his face between my legs and after another round between the sheets we ended up giving breakfast a miss and rushed straight to the first meeting.

The only thing that is keeping me from dropping off is the thought that the meeting with my family is next. A look at Tommy is telling me that he is also struggling. He is quieter than he was in the meetings yesterday and his expression lacks enthusiasm.

"This was all very interesting. Thank you so much. As I said, we will take all the proposals away and discuss them with our sales and legal teams." I have to suppress a chuckle. By sales team he means Frank the Head of Sales and by legal team he means the one local lawyer we occasionally ask to check our contracts.

When we get out of the building, Tommy's hand lands on my back and he guides me along the busy pavement.

"They were worse than yesterday," he says with frustration in his voice. "Did anyone read the brief we gave them? Our building is Victorian, and they give me lofty, sleek and modern." My tummy is in knots. When he sees my family's plans, he'll know I was involved. I should have told him yesterday. It was the perfect moment when he asked me about my past. But instead, I just closed up.

Tommy drops his hand from mine when we step into the glass building. I have been through the lobby a million times, yet it feels different now that I enter it as a customer.

The receptionist is new and she doesn't recognise me. Tommy gives his name and she hands over two visitor badges and directs us to the lift. We step into the lift and after the doors close, Tommy takes one of the stickers saying "Visitor" and sticks it to my chest. He taps it once, and a second time and I swear when he does it the third time, he swipes his thumb over my nipple.

"Tommy," I laugh and slap his hand away. He gives me a smirk and puts his visitor pass into his pocket. "No way, Mister, you have to wear it," I protest and reach in his pocket. I pull it out and peel it off before reaching out for his chest. He tries to avoid me and I end up chasing him through the lift.

"Tommy," I shout in fits of laughter just as the lift pings and the door opens. I turn and the smile on my face freezes. Tommy takes the sticker from me, crunches it up and puts it back in his jacket pocket.

Lee gives me an evil smile before directing his attention to Tommy.

"Thomas, it is so nice to meet in person," Lee says in his best sales rep voice before nodding at me. For business connections Tommy always uses his given name.

"Lee," Tommy greets him and shakes his hand. We follow my

51

brother to the boardroom. I don't recognise any of the staff that pass us, and I left less than one year ago. But the firm always had a problem with staff retention, thanks to how my dad and my brother treat them.

After Lee introduces us to some associated staff he has asked to join, we take a seat in the boardroom and Lee serves us tea. I am a little surprised that he is doing it himself. In the past, he would have had a secretary take care of us.

I am fighting hard to keep my anxiety in check. My leg is moving up and down nervously under the table and I feel every pointed look Lee gives me. Tommy glances at me occasionally and when they turn down the lights for the video presentation, he places a calming hand on my thigh. I try to draw strength from his touch.

I have to admit, they have done a great job at putting my drawings into a 3D model. It looks stunning and exactly how I had envisioned it. When the lights come back on there is excitement written all over Tommy's face, but he quickly catches himself.

He leans back and slowly flips through the pages of the folder with the proposal documents. All eyes are on him except for Lee's, which bore into me. I try to avoid him and luckily Tommy starts to ask questions.

When it is clear that there is nothing else to talk about, Tommy gives them the same run down of the next steps he gave everyone else and we leave. For one moment I was scared Lee would pull me aside but Tommy led me straight to the lift and so he didn't really have an opportunity to do so. I could feel his eyes following us though as we left the boardroom, and even Tommy's protective hand on my back couldn't calm me down.

When we step outside the sky is covered with dark clouds. I

pull my jacket close and we head towards the car parked in a car park nearby.

"What happened between you and your family?" Tommy breaks the silence.

"Nothing."

"Ella, please. You were anxious the whole time and your brother barely acknowledged you." Tommy stops me and gently turns my face so I have to look into his eyes. I take a deep breath and fight the tears.

"There's no place for me in my family. Just leave it at that. I—" This is the right moment to tell him, but I can't. He will be so angry with me and I will lose him. "Let's go, it will rain any minute." I grab his hand and drag him towards the car.

I only slow down when we step up to the BMW. My hair is damp because it had started to rain as we were approaching the multistorey car park. Tommy unlocks it and opens the boot. He throws his jacket on top of his garment bag and pulls his tie off. I grab a hair band from my bag and tie my hair back. I am about to walk to the passenger side of the car when Tommy's hand lands on my tummy.

"Ella—"

"Seriously, leave it."

"No, this is not about your family. What about us?" My heart starts to beat faster at his question.

"What about us?" I whisper. Is he going to tell me that we have to stop seeing each other? I know I had suggested we could just forget all about it when we return to Fellside, but having spent time with him last night, I don't think I will be able to.

"I don't want this to stop." His eyes are locked on me and I can see the same uncertainty that is in my mind.

"But?"

53

"But I would prefer if we don't make it public at work until we've had time to explore it." His eyes are pleading but he has nothing to fear. My lips tilt into a smile.

"So you want to keep seeing me?"

"Fuck, Ella, of course. I wanted nothing more for months. But I don't want you to feel like you are my dirty little secret."

"The way I see it, I kissed you first and I asked you to fuck me last night so I think you are my dirty little secret," I sass which causes Tommy to throw his head back in laughter. "But, joking aside, we're adults. I'm sure we can behave ourselves at work and in the evenings, when you can pull yourself away from work, you can come to mine. I have a nice little flat with only holiday lets as neighbours." I place a soft kiss on his mouth.

"Just do me one favour—"

"Yes?"

"No more pencil skirts. I can't guarantee I can keep my hands to myself otherwise." He presses his lips to my forehead and walks to the driver's side of the car.

"I make no such promises," I tease him with a smirk and pull the seatbelt over me. There are butterflies in my tummy and I have a cheesy smile on my lips but deep down there is a dark feeling trying to rise to the surface. *I need to tell him the truth. I need to!*

Chapter 9

I can hear Ella on the phone. The door to my office is closed, simply because otherwise I wouldn't get any work done. Ella and I have been secretly dating for two weeks now and I just can't get enough of her. I stay at her flat most nights and return to the hotel in the early morning. I am not sure what my staff think, but I am convinced that rumours are flying around about me having a new person in my life that keeps me out all night.

Only they haven't guessed yet that it's Ella who I spend my evenings with.

"Fuck," I mumble and rub the back of my neck. I desperately want to call her in so I can kiss her. That woman is like an addiction.

We have settled into a routine of being professional at work and then ripping each other's clothes off at home. It is crazy, exhilarating but also exhausting. I don't want to keep her a secret anymore. I want the world to see how amazing she is.

"Tommy," Ella says as she knocks on the door before opening it a gap. "Alex is here."

"Send him in." I give her a small smile which she returns before stepping aside. Alex glances at her and then me before smirking. He drops in the chair in front of my desk.

"I'll get some tea," Ella says and excuses herself.

"So, you did make a move," he grins knowingly.

"What are you doing here, Alex?" I ignore his question because I really don't have time for this. Me mooning over Ella has already put me behind schedule.

Alex doesn't answer and just crosses his arms defiantly in front of his chest. He is a bloody master in just stubbornly waiting until you spill your guts. He could work for MI5.

"Okay, yes, we are dating. But nobody in the hotel knows," I whisper and can't help it when a smile spreads over my face.

"You look happy." I sigh at Alex's statement.

"Very. Mate, I... I really can't describe it."

"No need. Don't forget I married the love of my life. I get it," he says before scratching his chest.

"So, what do you want? You didn't come all the way out here to chitchat."

"Rob called. His doctor said he is out for another eight weeks."

"Fuck!" My words echo around the room. Rob had an accident on a mission a few months back and his leg got badly damaged. With him out of action and Suzie about to give birth, our unit is on the verge of being understaffed. That means that if anyone is on holiday or ill we won't be called on.

"Why did he call you?" I'm the leader of the team; Rob should have spoken to me.

"He called me for advice on how to best tell you. I promised him I'd tell you because I have a solution." He scratches his left peck again.

"Why do you keep scratching yourself? Do you have a rash?"

"No, but this is kind of the reason why I am here. I have a tattoo and it's healing at the moment." He looks at me sheepishly.

"You have a tattoo?" I raise my eyebrow in question.

"Yes, why is that so surprising?"

"Well, for a start, I didn't know you were into tattoos."

"I wanted one for Emma and when the tattoo shop opened in the village—" I stop him mid-sentence when I can't hold back a chuckle.

"Are you telling me the conservative twats of the chamber of commerce allowed a tattoo shop to open in the village?"

Alex leans forward and whispers with a smirk on his face, "Smack bang in the middle right opposite the church." We look at each other for a minute before bursting into fits of laughter.

"Boy, how did the WI take it?"

"Don't know yet. I think they are still in their war council. Anyway. Ryan, the guy who runs the shop, and I got talking when he was doing my tattoo. He was a climber in his youth. He has started again now he moved to Fellside and I thought we could take him on as a trainee."

"I take it he is interested."

"Yes, and he understands the time commitment. He has someone working with him who can cover."

I lean back in my chair. Having another person on the team would definitely be great, even if it is just a trainee. He will only be able to do the basic tasks in the beginning, but it will be a great help nonetheless. And it would solve the staffing problem.

"Why not," I shrug. "Bring him to the meeting next week and I'll have a chat with him."

"Excellent, well, I'll leave you to your work."

"You know you could have just called me."

"Your head housekeeper sent for me; something about a broken headboard or something. I'm heading to housekeeping now, but I wanted to talk to you first." Alex is our go-to carpenter when we need repairs at the hotel. Not because he is my friend, but because he is the best and most reliable.

"Thanks, mate."

"No worries."

"Alex," I stop him as he is about to open the door, "What tattoo did you get?"

"A blossom with Emma's name in it." He has a loved up look on his face. Yes, he definitely found the love of his life. The minute I think this, Ella's face pops into my mind.

"How very romantic of you," I chuckle but he knows I am just teasing.

"Hey, I'm Mr Romantic," he replies with a smirk before waving goodbye and closing the door behind him.

I stare out of the window. I love Greenview Manor but lately I've been wondering if there isn't more to life.

"Tommy?" Ella's soft voice brings me back to reality. I swivel in my chair and see her standing in the door.

"Ella, would you mind coming in and closing the door please?" I ask in my best boss voice. A small smile tilts her lips and she does as I asked. I hold out my hand to her and she crosses the room to give me hers. I pull her into my lap and the minute she is in my arms I feel relaxed and content.

"Tommy, " she giggles quietly, "What if someone comes?"

"They wouldn't enter my office without knocking," I whisper against the skin of her neck before placing soft kisses there. A small moan escapes her when I hit the spot right behind her ear that she likes so much.

"Are you going to come over today?" she asks before sliding her hand over the front of my trouser where my hard cock is straining to get out and play.

"A thousand angry hotel guests couldn't keep me away from you."

Ella giggles and then slaps me tenderly on the chest.

"Hush, don't jinx it. We have been complaint free for four weeks." It doesn't matter how perfect a hotel is, things will go wrong and guests make sure you know about it. And even if nothing goes wrong, some still think "The guest is the king" and behave like my staff are their personal servants. It sometimes amazes me how people who are perfectly decent in normal life can turn into complete and utter arseholes the minute they book themselves into a hotel. Common decency and politeness are left at home.

"I don't want to talk about our guests now," I mumble before pulling her to me for a deep kiss. My fingers slide up her thigh and under her pencil skirt.

"Tommy!" She softly pushes off me and stands up. "Not here, you naughty man." She tries to reprimand me, but the lust in her eyes tells me otherwise.

"I told you, if you wear these skirts, I can't be held responsible for anything." She laughs and steps up to me again. She cups my face and places one long kiss on my lips.

"That has to be enough until later."

"Fine," I grumble.

"Well, Boss, I am heading home for the day because it's five o'clock," she says loudly even if there is nobody around, before winking at me. As she opens the door, I can see Sheila hovering outside.

"Sheila, do you need anything?" I call out. She gives Ella a smile before stepping into my office looking a little nervous. "Is everything okay?" I ask again.

"Yeah, yes, sure. I have the staff rotas for you." She holds out a few pieces of paper. Yes, we are still old school here but Sheila recently showed me an app we can use and I signed off the order for it yesterday.

"Thanks." When she doesn't move, I add, "Anything else?"

"I—" She stops herself, walks up to the door and closes it. "Tommy, I have been working with you for three years now and I hope we have a relationship where I can be open with you?"

"Sure," I lean back but I am getting nervous. Is she planning to resign? Sheila is a superstar and losing her would be a massive blow.

"Are you and Ella dating?"

"What?" Shock must be showing on my face because she nervously rubs her hands together.

"It's just that you are different since the two of you are back from Manchester. Or should I say, you are back to your cheerful self. Ever since Ella joined us you were so moody; staff had started to talk thinking that the hotel is in financial trouble and that they could get fired any minute."

I take a deep breath. I hadn't realised how I had come across.

"Shit, I don't want staff to worry. I'll talk to them." Sheila nods.

"You should talk to them, but you should tell them the truth."

"About?"

"You and Ella."

"Sheila—"

"No, Tommy, please, as a friend, let me tell you. Nobody will care. You didn't date her before she came here. She has no advantage by dating you, it's not like you can promote her above anyone. She is widely liked. So, nobody will care. If anything, they'll be happy for you. But by being honest you stop any rumours from spreading. I mean, I noticed because I'm observant," she giggles, "but in the long run you won't be able to hide it. Better out in the open and everyone will forget about it."

I run one hand through my hair. "We were waiting until we know if it's serious."

"From what I've observed, you're both smitten."

"How? We were so careful."

Sheila laughs out loud.

"Please! Whenever she walks into a room, your eyes seek her out. You watch her interact with others and you have this small smile on your lips. And your door has been closed every time I've come to the office in the last two weeks." I should be embarrassed but all I can do is smile.

"I'll talk to her and we'll announce it in the next few days. I'm just worried staff will think I am a hypocrite."

"Because of Ian?" Anna caught the head chef making in-appropriate advances on a female apprentice whilst I was in Manchester and fired him on the spot.

"Tommy, don't be silly. That's completely different. Ian was a sleaze who behaved highly inappropriately toward a number of women. I don't need to know the details of your relationship to know that Ella wants this too."

"She does."

Sheila nods and gets off the chair.

"Trust me, nobody will judge the two of you because everyone will see this isn't a seedy affair but a lot more."

"Thanks, Sheila."

"Not at all. That's my job."

"What? Watching out for my love life?" I chuckle.

"No, supporting you in making this hotel a success. The team holds you in high regard, Tommy. We have one of the lowest rates of staff turnover in the area and that's because people love working for you. Everyone will be happy for you and then move on. And I'll make sure they don't gossip," she says with a final laugh before leaving.

My eyes drop to the expansion plans on my desk. My lawyer had a look at the proposal from Ella's family and found a few points in the contract to query but otherwise it looks fine. I really should be preparing a reply to them but instead I push the papers into one pile, grab my mobile and my car keys. I need to be with Ella.

I walk pass reception to let them know that I'm leaving for the day and head to my car. As the car rolls along the driveway my heart starts hammering faster. She left less than an hour ago, but I miss her already.

Chapter 10

Ella

I pull the towel into a tight turban on my head to keep my wet hair from dripping. The bedroom looks a bit like a bomb site with Tommy's bag in the corner overflowing with clothes. I reach for some T-shirts that seem to be fresh and put them on a hanger in my wardrobe.

He spends almost every night here and has made it a habit to leave clothes at mine to change into. And it makes me weirdly happy. It feels domestic, it feels permanent. I throw some of his dirty clothes in the laundry hamper in the corner and add my clothes from today on top of it, before putting on some yoga pants and casual top.

I am past that stage where I feel embarrassed about not wearing a bra in front of Tommy. He has seen my breasts plenty of times, and he knows they are not as perky as those of a twenty-year-old, but he doesn't seem to mind. I grin. *No, he doesn't mind at all.*

I drag the hamper to the kitchen and load the washing machine with our clothes. My hips are swaying along to the music filtering through the speaker on the kitchen counter. I love some music when I do housework. I am just wondering if I should drive to the supermarket to do some shopping when the flat door opens. Tommy has a habit of working late so I have given him a key to my flat to let himself in late at night.

My eyes flit to the clock on the wall. It is only just after six. He is early.

"Hey, babe," he says before dropping two full shopping bags on the kitchen counter.

I lean back against the cabinets.

"What's all this?"

"I saw food was low and I thought we could cook together," he grins at me. But then something changes in his face. He crosses the distance between us and smashes his lips on mine. His kiss is urgent.

"Fuck, you look hot," he mumbles in between kisses. I laugh out loud and softly push him off me.

"Tommy, I am wearing yoga pants, towel turban and no underwear. I don't think hot is the right word."

"You are right, you look amazingly hot," he says; his eyes are dark and full of desire. "Wait, did you say no underwear?"

"Maybe." I can feel the heat in my cheeks.

"Fuck, let me see." He reaches out and grabs the waistband of my yoga pants.

"Tommy!" I laugh out loud but I don't stop him when he pushes my trousers over my hips. The soft material slides to the floor. Before I can say anything else he gently places me on the kitchen counter and steps between my legs. My towel turban falls off and my damp hair uncoils.

"I need you, Ella," he whispers with his warm lips sliding over my neck whilst his fingers dip between my legs.

"I'm not stopping you," I reply and Tommy growls deeply. He places my legs around his hips and when I lock them, he lifts me off the counter and carries me towards the bedroom.

"I'll tell you now, Ella, this won't be slow or tender. I need you hard and fast today."

"Hard and fast is good," I moan, nibbling on his earlobe. He loves it when I do that.

When we get to the bedroom, he drops me onto the bed. The minute I hit the mattress, he reaches for his trousers, unbuckles his belt and slides them down. I take my T-shirt off and then lay there waiting on the bed for this amazing man.

After taking off his clothes, Tommy crawls onto the bed and whispers in my ear, "Turn around." As I move to be on my front, he pushes a pillow under my hips and starts kissing a trail down my spine.

"Fuck, Tommy, you said hard and fast. I need you in me now," I complain. My fingers are grabbing the sheet underneath me tightly. I hear the familiar sound of a condom package being ripped open.

Tommy slides his body along mine and then enters me from behind. I love the angle he gets when he takes me this way. His hands slide along my arms and our fingers lock. He anchors us to the mattress and then pushes into me ferociously. With every thrust his hard cock hits my G-spot. My orgasm builds too fast. I don't want this to be over, but Tommy doesn't slow down. He groans and sucks on my neck.

"You feel so amazing, Ella. Being with you is the best feeling in the world," he whispers in my ear. Leave it to this man to say the sweetest thing in the hottest moment.

"Tommy!" I cry out as the orgasm washes over me. He keeps moving until he finds his own release and his thrusts keep my orgasm raging until he slumps down on me and stills.

He rolls to the side so his weight is no longer on me and takes me with him. His arms close around me and he holds me tight. This right here is my favourite place in the world.

* * *

"Baby, I forgot to get milk yesterday," Tommy calls out from the kitchen. He was supposed to make us a cup of tea whilst I get ready for work.

"We can always have a cuppa at work, " I call back. Tommy appears in the bedroom door. He is already in his shirt and trousers, but his tie is hanging loosely around his neck.

"That's fine, I'll just pop to the corner shop," he says before placing a small kiss on my neck.

"Okay," I smile and he leaves me alone in the bedroom. I reach for one of my smart black trousers. I need to get some work done today and Tommy tends to distract me more when I wear my skirts. I feel the familiar warmth spreading through me. It's the feeling I get every time I think about him and me. He wants to tell the staff today. We talked about it a lot last night, and I can see the point. Frankly, I don't want to hide anymore.

The doorbell pulls me from my thoughts. I pick up my suit jacket from where I had put it on the bed and walk to the flat door. I pull it open expecting a sheepish looking Tommy because he has forgotten his keys yet again.

Instead, a strong hand grabs me around the throat and presses me against the nearest wall. I hear the door slam shut.

"Lee, you're hurting me," I croak out. My head stings from where it made contact with the wall, and his fingers press painfully into the sides of my neck.

"You don't even know how much I can hurt you. What the fuck are you playing, Ella? Why have we not received the yes on the project yet?"

"He's still working on your proposal," I sputter. My fingers grab his hand and I try to push him off me. Reluctantly, he lets go of me and I slump against the wall.

"Ella, I've fucking had enough. We need this deal. We need the signature on the paper by the end of the week or the bank won't extend our loan. Make it happen," Lee shouts and points his fingers at me. I try to move away from him but he has me cornered against the wall.

"Do you fucking understand?" he roars. I nod just as the door opens.

Everyone freezes for a moment.

"What's going on?" Tommy asks.

Lee's eyes dart between me and Tommy. Concern briefly crosses his face before he takes another step back.

"Thomas," he greets Tommy, "I was just in the village so I popped by to say hello to my sister." His tone is cold but not unpleasant. His stance is wide and his arms are crossed in front of his chest. "We haven't heard back from you on the proposal yet." There is a smirk on his face. "But I guess you have been busy." When he says the last word, his eyes look back at me where I am leaning against the wall.

"We'll let everyone know in the next few days," Tommy replies politely but the tone of his voice makes it sound like a threat.

"I see... I didn't know you and Ella are living together," Lee looks straight into Tommy's eyes. My heart hammers in my chest and the fear I feel is making it hard to breathe.

"We're not," I whisper drawing the attention of both of them to me. Lee slowly turns his head and his eyes bore into mine.

"Well, it's not really my business," he finally says. "I'll see you later." He puts an emphasis on the word later. Tommy, who had been blocking the flat door, takes a step aside, allowing Lee to leave.

When the door clicks shut and I know he is gone, I can't hold my tears back any longer. I slide downwards until I end up sitting on the floor sobbing.

"Ella?" Tommy's voice is laced with confusion and worry.

"I'm so sorry, Tommy. I am so sorry," I cry out in between sobs. I'm not looking at him, instead my head is buried in my hands. Tommy scoops me up and carries me to the sofa where he holds me close.

"Tell me what happened."

"I should have told you the truth," I whisper. I can feel him stiffen under me.

"What do you mean?" he asks. He sounds more agitated now. I lift my head from his chest. I notice that my hands are shaking and I press them together in the hope to make it stop.

"Lee wants me to convince you to choose my family's business," I say in a small voice. Tommy just stares at me and says nothing. He lifts me of his lap and stands up.

"What are you saying Ella. I don't—" He paces the living room before heading for the kitchen and returning with a piece of kitchen roll. He holds it out to me and I take the paper towel with shaking hands. I wipe my tears away and blow my nose, but I am not sure what good it will do as my tears are still rolling uncontrollably over my cheeks.

Tommy is just staring down at me. "I don't believe this. Explain it again to me. When I sent out the tender invitations you said you had nothing to do with your family's business!"

He looks confused and stressed.

"Lee... Lee made me draw up the plans for the hotel because he knew I would know what you would like. And then he wanted me to convince you to sign the proposal. Tommy, I'm sorry. I'm so sorry."

"You took this job to manipulate me? And what for? To serve a family you told me you don't feel you belong to?" He crosses his arms in front of his chest and his facial expression has changed from confusion to anger. His last sentence hits me hard.

"No, no. I didn't know anything about the expansion when I accepted the job. I told you that I moved here to get away from my family."

"Then what? You started this relationship," he puts the word relationship in air quotes, "to get me to do what you want?"

I shake my head. Of course, he would think that. That's exactly what it looks like, but I would have hoped he would trust me more.

"No, I kept telling Lee I wouldn't do that to you. But Lee kept threatening me. I told him you have to make up your own mind. But—"

"But what?" He sounds cold and hurt.

"I did draw up the plans they showed you, there's no denying it. Lee's ideas are crap which is why the firm is in trouble. I did most of the planning behind the scenes in the past, and Lee took credit for my work. Both my brother and my dad kept telling me that I should stop being self-centred when I asked that projects have my name on them. It was all for the family. That's why I left. And when Lee found out about this project, he and dad, well—"

Tommy's glare makes me cry more. I am shaking and I feel like something is dying in me. I stand up and walk to him. I put

69

my hand on his arm but he moves away from me.

"In short, you used your knowledge of me to draw up plans that you knew I would like to give your family's firm an advantage."

"Yes," I whisper. "And no. When I drew the plans, I wanted you to have the build you had envisioned. I love this hotel and I wanted it to be right. But, yes, I knew it would also help my family. I hoped they would then leave me alone."

"Fuck, Ella!" There are so many emotions in his voice but the anger and hurt are unmissable.

"I wanted to tell you a number of times over the last couple of weeks, but I was worried you would despise me."

"Ella—" His fingers roam through his hair and he looks to be in pain. "Ella, I... what is this?" He stops what he wanted to say. Instead he tenderly takes my chin between his thumb and forefinger and turns my head.

"What is what?"

"You have bruises on your neck. They weren't there earlier." My hand shoots up to cover them. "Ella, how did you get the bruises?" His eyes are locked on me.

"It doesn't matter."

"It matters to me. Was it Lee?"

I don't reply and that is answer enough for Tommy.

"I am going to fucking kill him," he growls before walking towards the door. I grab his arm and pull him back.

"No, Tommy, leave it."

"You need to at least report him to the police."

"He's family." I can't report Lee. He and my family will never let me forget this. Never.

"Fuck, Ella, no. That is not an excuse."

"Please, Tommy," I plead with him. "Tell them today that

you won't hire them and he will be out of our life, your life."

Tommy's hands are in fists and his breathing is laboured.

"Please. I'll pack my stuff and move somewhere else and you don't have to deal with any of us again."

He puts his hands on my shoulders.

"What are you talking about?"

"I know I hurt you and I am so sorry that I didn't tell you the truth, but please believe me: none of my feelings were a lie. I know what I did is unforgivable, but I just want you to know that." More tears are flowing over my face. I feel tired and empty. I just want to curl up in a ball somewhere and cry until the pain stops. Silence fills the room as we look into each other's eyes.

"Ella, I love you," Tommy finally says. "Am I happy that you didn't tell me the truth? No! But I can now see why." He slides his fingers over the spot where Lee had pressed his fingers into my neck. "Baby, I love you." He places his forehead against mine. The anger has disappeared from his face. "Just promise me from now on, no more lies. If you are scared, you'll tell me."

"I am so scared, Tommy," I whisper.

"What about, baby?"

"Of losing you." I sob and he finally pulls me in his arms. I slide my hands around his waist and melt into his embrace.

"You're not losing me, Ella."

Chapter 11

Tommy

"Mr Hunter, Mr Compton, they are ready for you now," the young secretary says. I drop my phone back into my pocket and Nick and I rise from our chairs in the waiting room of Lee's company. I have been fighting my anger since Lee left Ella's flat but I can still feel it burning in my guts.

I could have sent them an email rejecting the project but I needed to see them in person to make sure they leave Ella alone. Nick has tagged along as a witness but also to stop me in case I need to be held back. Any of the FMR guys would have been here with me, but Nick, who is a teacher, is on half term at the moment, so it was easy for him to join me on a meeting during the week.

"Thomas, it is so good to see you again." Despite his words, Lee doesn't sound happy to see me again. His eyes are coldly staring at me when he holds out his hand. I grab it and squeeze it as hard as I can. For a brief moment he shows the pain on his face but then he is in control again. Oh, the things I would like to do to this man. I had to promise Ella to leave the police out of it and to not engage in any physical violence. This family has put her through so much but they still have a hold on her. It's some weird form of Stockholm syndrome and I want to get her some help to work through this.

Truthfully, she didn't need to worry. I am not a violent person. I don't think I have ever had a fist fight, not even in school. But for Lee I would make an exception. Nobody hurts Ella. Nobody.

"Let me introduce you to my father." The older man in the room rises from the chair and comes over.

"Pleasure, and who is your associate?" the older gentleman asks. He looks very much like Lee. I can't see anything in his face that would remind me of Ella.

"This is my friend Nick." I leave it at that and neither Lee nor his father ask more, even if I can see that they are curious.

"Should we take a seat?" Lee tries to guide us towards the boardroom table where a few staff members sit, just like the last time.

"I don't think that will be necessary," I stop him. "I am just here to tell you that your firm won't get the contract." The fake smile drops from both their faces. I can feel Nick taking a small step closer. He is telling me he is here.

"I don't work with people who use and abuse their own family members."

"But—" Lee tries to interject.

"No," I shout and my voice booms through the meeting room. "You listen." I take a step closer and Nick is again right behind me. "If you ever so much as look in Ella's direction again, I will go to the police even if I have to break I promise I made her."

I wait but neither of them says anything. The other people in the room shift nervously.

73

"Well, fuck you and your hotel," Lee finally hisses.

"Mr Hunter, I think it is best if you leave now." I can see anger in the old man's face and I am almost losing it. Neither of them is showing any kind of remorse.

"She's your daughter; you should have protected her," I shout before turning to Lee, "She is your sister, how can you treat her like that?"

"Please leave," Ella's father says. "I don't want to do business with someone who accuses us of practices like this. Especially not someone who is abusing his position to seduce a vulnerable woman. I wonder what your guests and staff would say about that," he grins at me like he just landed a blow.

I feel Nick's hand on my shoulder and I'm glad he is there. I try to calm my breathing because I am close to a heart attack with the rage flowing through me.

"My staff know that I'm in love with your daughter." I can see his self-assured smile slip for a minute. "And my guests only care if their poached eggs are runny." Nick snorts behind me. I'm not even lying. I rounded up all our staff yesterday and I made a very brief speech. They all cheered and then went back to business. Sheila was right. Nobody really cared.

"Don't threaten us because you won't win that game. I have way more information on you than you will ever have on me. Not that I have ever behaved in a way that could be harmful to my or Ella's future, like you have. Stay away from Ella, best stay away from Fellside. Only because she asked me, I haven't called the police...yet. But if I ever see you in Fellside again, I will get the police involved." I point at them both before turning around and stalking to the door of the meeting room.

"It was not nice to meet you," Nick chuckles behind me to everyone in the boardroom before catching up with me.

"Tommy, take a few breaths before you keel over," Nick demands.

"Can you fucking believe them?" I shout, causing a young guy who is standing in front of the lift to drop a pile of papers. He quickly scoops them up and scurries away.

"No. But then I can't imagine threatening my own sister."

"Your sister would kick your arse if you tried," I reply as we step into the lift.

"True," he chuckles, "But seriously, Tommy, I could never do something like that. They are two twisted fucks and not worth your breath."

"Let's go back. I need to see her."

"Fucking hell, a four hour round journey just to yell at two first grade arseholes. At least get me a coffee," he chuckles.

"I'll get you a takeaway," I laugh before adding, "I need to see her."

* * *

Nick drops me off at the hotel and I jog up the back stairs to my flat. After sharing our relationship with the staff, I asked her to stay with me until I felt confident that Lee wouldn't trouble her again. To my surprise, she agreed without putting up a fight. This makes me think she's still scared, even though she tried to reassure me that Lee would back off.

"Babe," I call out as I enter the flat.

"Bathroom," Ella replies. I drop my jacket on the chair, toe off my shoes and follow the voice.

"Can I come in?" I ask.

"Sure," she giggles. I open the door and steam hits me in the face. The room is dimly lit with only two of the wall lights on.

Ella is sitting in my large bathtub covered by bath foam with a book in her hand. She gives me a half smile.

"Hope that's okay? I thought it might help me relax." She looks at me concerned.

"Of course. Can I join you?" Her eyes light up and that's all I need to strip off my clothes. When I step up to the tub, she drops the book on the floor. The warm water immediately calms me as I slide in behind her, but I only relax fully once she leans back against my chest and I can put my arms around her.

"How did it go?" she asks with worry in her voice. She let me leave after I had promised that I wouldn't call the police.

"I hate them," I hiss. She doesn't reply to my statement. Instead, she starts to gently stroke my arm. "Your father threatened to give our relationship away to create some scandal."

"What scandal? Who the heck would care?" She laughs bitterly.

"That's what I told him. I—" I take a deep breath.

"Tommy, tell me."

"I am sorry that you belong to a family like that."

"I never really belonged in that family," she whispers, and then presses tighter against me.

"I am so sorry about everything you have been through."

"Thank you. And thank you for standing with me, even after I lied to you."

"Ella—" She turns and presses a soft kiss on my mouth.

"Make love to me, Tommy."

Chapter 12

Ella

I glance at my watch as I walk up to Tommy's BMW parked at the back of the FMR building. He had to attend a team meeting and I used the time to do some shopping, but he should be almost finished. I place the large heavy bag with my hiking boots next to the car. Tommy wants to take me up on Fellside Horseshoe next weekend and I wanted to make sure I have the right footwear. I will struggle enough as it is because my fitness is not the best, so at least I want to make sure my feet will be comfortable.

"You bitch." I recognise Lee's voice but before I can react, he grabs my hair and pulls me with him. He drags me near the wall of the house, out of sight of the road. The only way someone would see us here is if they walked out of the building.

"Lee, please, let me go," I plead.

"No. It's about time you get what you deserve. I have been following you all morning and now I finally get you alone."

My eyes dart around but I can't see anyone. I notice a window open on the upper floor. Maybe if I scream someone will hear me. I open my mouth but Lee puts his hand over it and presses me up against the wall.

"No, no, Ella, no calling for your knight in shining armour." I can smell alcohol on his breath. And it's not just a hint, he smells like a brewery. Panic rises in me. Lee is unpredictable at the best of times, but when he is drunk there is no bargaining with him. When I was younger I ended up in hospital with a broken cheek bone thanks to him. My mum told the doctors a random man attacked me on the way home from the pub. Afterwards she said that it must have been my mistake. I must have provoked him because otherwise he'd never have hit me that hard.

"We are ruined and all just because of you. Dad is furious. You already spread your legs to him, what was the big issue? We just asked you for a small favour but no, you couldn't do that for us." His hand slips a little and is now only half covering my mouth. I use the opportunity to open my lips and bite his hand hard. He yelps out in pain and pulls it back.

"You stupid cow," he shouts and I feel an explosion on my face before his fingers squeeze my windpipe again. I am gasping for air.

"Hey!" I hear someone shout. Lee's hand drops from my throat. I can finally breathe again.

"What the fuck did I tell you about showing your face here," Tommy booms. Lee takes some steps back and Tommy is next to me in instant. When he sees my face where, judging by the pain radiating from my cheek, Lee's hand imprint must be visible, he turns around to face my brother.

"You fucker, I'll kill you," he growls. Lee just glares at him. Before Tommy can start towards my brother, I reach out and softly grab Tommy's arm.

"Don't, he's not worth it," I whisper. He looks at me. I can see the anger and the pain in his face. This time he's not angry with me, but he's in pain because of what's happened to me. He gently cups my face.

"Baby, I can't let him get—"

"Watch out!" a voice shouts from behind Tommy. We both look at Lee and see him charging forward something silver in his hand. Tommy turns back to me and cages me against the wall protecting me with his whole body. Our eyes are locked and in slow motion I wait for him to react to Lee slamming into him but he doesn't. Instead, there is a scream next to us, and a tall, tattooed guy is pinning Lee to the floor.

"Get off me!" My brother tries to wriggle free. "That's assault!"

"Shut up," the guy sitting on him says and presses Lee's head against the tarmac. His bicep, which is covered in tribal symbols, flexes under the power he's using to restrain Lee. "What do you call what you just did to her?" he hisses at Lee.

"I did nothing to her. Ella, tell him." He must be delusional. Nick kicks the knife lying on the floor away and kneels down next to Lee to pin his legs down.

"Well, sadly for you there are two CCTV cameras up there, I'm pretty sure they'll tell a different story," Alex replies calmly as he puts his phone in his pocket. He looks at Tommy and adds, "Police will be here in five minutes."

"Tommy, take care of your girl. Nick and Alex can help me with this fucker," the tattooed guy says and gives us a reassuring smile.

Tommy nods at his team and guides me into the building. He takes me to a small kitchen on the upper floor of the FMR centre. Without saying a word, he lifts me to sit on one of the counters before grabbing an ice pack from a small fridge freezer. He wraps it in a tea towel and gently presses it against my face.

"How are you?" he finally breaks the silence. His voice is quiet but there is an edge to it. I take a deep breath and wait for the tears to come, but there are none.

"Tommy, I need to tell the police," I finally whisper. I know I said I wouldn't but I have to. I can't live like this anymore and I can't risk Tommy getting hurt either. Enough is enough.

"Yes, baby, you do and I'll come with you." Tommy looks relieved that he doesn't have to fight me on it. Ever since the incident in my flat he has been trying to get me to go to the police, but something held me back. Was it the shame or fear, or maybe the knowledge that if I take that step then I definitely no longer have a family? I don't know. Maybe it was a combination of all three.

"Thank you." I don't need to explain what I'm thankful for. He put himself in harm's way to protect me. I don't even want to think about what could have happened if the others hadn't stopped Lee. But Tommy didn't hesitate. He put his life on the line for me. A sob escapes me.

"Any time. I love you, Ella, and I'll do anything to make sure you are safe." I nod at his words.

"Who was the guy who stopped Lee?" I ask.

"That's Ryan. We were deciding if he can join the team as a trainee and I think he just qualified." He steps between my legs and I snuggle up against him.

"How are you feeling?"

"Hurt, sad, but also relieved. I am sorry I dragged you into all this drama."

"I'm not. I don't care what happens in your life, the only thing I care about is that I'm part of it." A lone tear rolls over my cheek. This time it's a happy tear.

"Sorry to interrupt." Alex has appeared in the doorway. "The police are outside and they would like a word with both of you. I'll send them upstairs if that's okay?" Tommy's eyes remained on me as Alex was talking, but now he turns his head.

"Yeah, that's fine," he replies. Alex nods and pushes himself away from the doorway and turns.

"Oh, and Alex," Tommy shouts after his friend. When Alex looks at him, he adds, "Tell Ryan welcome to the team." They both grin at each other.

* * *

Tommy turns off the main light before joining me in bed. He slides under the duvet and pulls me into his arms. As I reach out for the bedside lamp to switch it off he stops me.

"Wait, I know you are tired, baby, but you have barely spoken since we've been back. Are you okay?"

Am I okay? How can I be when I just filed a police report against my brother for physical assault? After the police took our statements at the FMR building they asked us to come to the station to take a full account from me. I was there for two hours telling them everything that's happened.

Tommy wasn't allowed to be with me, and I would have needed his strength. But he was waiting outside for me. The minute I walked from the room he pulled me into his arms and I felt safe again.

"I don't know," I admit. We had promised each other that there would be no more secrets. He frowns and pulls me closer. He is lying on his side and his head is propped up on one hand. His other hand is drawing circles on my tummy

"I think we should take a holiday. Just you and me. Two weeks relaxing in the sun somewhere," he finally says. I study his face. He looks sincere which makes me burst out laughing.

"Why are you laughing?"

"Because you can barely find time for lunch. How are you going to make time for a holiday?"

"I have been thinking. I'll promote Sheila to General Manager. Hell, when Mr Sinder owned the hotel, he hired me as a general manager. And it worked well. He carried the big decisions and I took care of the day-to-day problems. I think it's time to do the same."

I cup his face and softly stroke his cheek. "Are you sure you're ready for this?"

"Ella, I've been working since I was sixteen. In the last five years I've barely had a day off. I'm the one who constantly cancels on my friends."

"They understand."

"Yeah, they do. They've never held my no-shows against me. But they're my family and I want to make time for them. And I need to make time for you. And I need to make time for me. I'm tired, Ella."

I smile at him. "In that case, it sounds like a very good plan. What about the extension?"

"Well," he bends forward and places soft kisses on my collarbone, "I'll speak with the bank and ask if we can delay the loan by six months. This gives us enough time...," he places a kiss between my breast, "... for us to go on a nice holiday and for me to train Sheila up. Oh, and for you to draw up new plans."

I place my hands on either side of his head and make him look at me.

"Me?"

"Yes, regardless of what happened the plans you did were part

82

of your father's company's proposal, so legally we could get into trouble using them. But I'm pretty confident you can come up with an even better concept," he grins. I sit up, excitement coursing through me.

"Actually, I was thinking. If you are interested, how about adding a few self-contained cottages down at the lake, with a main building including a yoga studio and a library? We could offer it as a retreat area. We had an enquiry from a group of authors last week who want to hold a writing retreat and that's how I came up with the idea. They could shut off down there and if they need a little bit more luxury they can walk up to the hotel for dinner."

Tommy just stares at me.

"If you hate the idea, that's okay," I mumble, sliding back under the duvet.

"No, baby, I love the idea," he assures me before placing a soft kiss on my lips. "I was just wondering what I did to deserve you in my life." With this, he pulls me back to him and kisses me long and hard. I'm pretty sure I should ask the same question but I'm just glad we found to each other.

Epilogue

Tommy

"Ella, look at me. You can do this, baby." My voice is as calm as it can be. Ella is shaking in my arms. Her eyes are filled with tears and her fingers are digging into my back.

"Are you ready?" the instructor asks. Ella presses her head against my neck and shakes her head, but I give him a smile and a thumbs up. Ella is strapped to me and I slowly walk us to the edge of the platform.

Ella and I are in New Zealand. Our short two-week holiday in the sun turned into a four-week trip around New Zealand in a VW minibus. We have been whale watching, been on some amazing hikes, and have camped at some beautiful spots. Now we are on the South Island for Ella to fulfil one of her bucket list dreams: bungee jumping. She made me swear on my life yesterday that I'd make her do it regardless of how scared she felt.

"Baby, look at me please," I whisper. Ella meets my eyes, a lone tear running down her cheek. She is hyperventilating.

"Breathe, baby. Copy me." I take a deep breath, and another. She tries to copy me and her breathing slows a little.

"Are you sure you want to do this?"

"No, Tommy, you promised," she says between deep breaths.

"Okay, let's go, baby." I lift her in my arms and she locks her legs around my hips. I stand on the edge, my heart racing like I just finished a marathon, stealing a quick glance at her—she's a mix of wide-eyed excitement and trembling nerves, and it tugs at my heart.

"We got this," I say confidently and give her a big smile. She nods but her nails digging into my back tell me that the fear is still here. "I'll keep you safe, baby."

And then, I jump. We are hurtling into the unknown together, the world below turning into a swirling sea of colours. The wind roars in my ears, drowning out everything else. As the bungee cord bounces us back, a wild cocktail of love and exhilaration courses through me. Our fingers weave together and in that suspended, weightless moment, it hits me—this jump isn't just about the fall. It's about us, about discovering something incredible in each other's company, something that transforms the simplest moments into memories we'll cherish forever. And I now know for sure that I want a forever with her.

* * *

I watch Ella in the side mirror as she tries to guide me into the little parking spot. We are on the shore of a beautiful mountain lake and after handing over a generous tip, we were allocated the most remote and most romantic spot on the campsite. There is not a soul around. Ella had read about the campsite on an online blog and I was determined to get that spot for us.

When she gives me the stop sign I cut the engine put the handbrake on and jump from the vehicle.

"What an amazing view," Ella says as she steps up to me. I put my hand around her shoulder, pull her into my side and place a kiss on her head.

"It's even better because you're here." This is week three of our holiday and I haven't checked in with the hotel even once. Sheila was over the moon with her promotion and we quickly worked out a system that works for both of us. I have full confidence in her.

"Come on, Romeo: dinner." Ella pats my abs and walks back to the minibus. She slides open the side door and jumps onto the mattress. Frankly, there isn't much in that minibus. We store most of our stuff at the rear of it and the main section is taken over by a massive mattress. We eat on it, sleep on it, and have had incredible sex on it in some of the most remote spots we've visited. Luckily this minibus has curtains on the windows, even if it doesn't have much else. It's simple but we absolutely love it. So much so that we extended our holiday by a fourth week. Am I concerned? Not a bit.

I sit down next to Ella and take my take away box from her. We picked up burgers and chips on the way here. They are cold now but we're watching an amazing sunset over a crystal-clear lake. Who cares if the burger is cold.

We don't say much. We just watch the spectacle nature is providing us. When we have finished our meal Ella stuffs our containers in a shopping bag that is hanging from the open door and slides back onto the mattress where she places pillows against the opposite side wall of the minibus. This way we can lie down and still watch the sunset.

I take my shoes off and crawl over to her. When I settle in next to Ella, she places her head on my chest and we just lie there in silence. This is what happiness feels like. Could I be any happier? Yes, I could.

"Ella?"

"Shh," she whispers. Her hand is under my shirt on my stomach. She loves to feel my skin even if we just lie there and read or watch a movie.

Since she won't let me talk I decide to speak with actions. I reach into my pocket and put the little blue box onto my stomach right above where her hand is currently placed under my shirt. Ella stiffens, then lifts her head and looks at me.

"What's that."

"I'm not allowed to talk," I joke.

"Tommy! What is this?"

I take the box, sit up and pull her with me.

"Ella, I didn't have a life until you. Rob joked once that work was my true love but I know now I was just hiding behind it. You brought laughter, happiness, and joy into my world and I can't imagine not having you in my life. So—"

"Tommy, we have only known each other for what, just under a year? We've only been together for a few months."

"So?"

"So, aren't there rules? Shouldn't we date first for a year, a year and a half, then live together for a while and then—"

"Ella, you've been living with me since the incident." That's what we call it. The incident. "And who made these rules? All I know is that I need you in my life. Every day, every night. I love you." I open the box and show her the platinum ring with small sapphires. Ella hates diamonds, but she loves blue.

"Will you marry me, Ella?"

She sobs and looks from the ring to me.

"Yes, yes I will," she whispers before pulling me in for a kiss. After I slide the ring on her finger, she leans against me.

"Oh no, we missed the best part of the sunset," she exclaims, and I look at the lake. The sun has set behind the horizon and now all that is left is dusk.

"Well maybe we just have to stay another day. And for now, we can—" I crawl to the door and slide it close. "For now,we can celebrate our engagement. Time for my dessert, baby."

WANT MORE?

Download this bonus chapter and find out what the future holds for Tommy and Ella.

Get it here:
https://BookHip.com/LJKTGVH

THANK YOU

Thank you for taking the time to read Build with Me. Please spare a minute to leave a review on Amazon and Goodreads! Even a short sentence or two helps.

STAY IN TOUCH

Never miss a new release: Sign up for my newsletter to be the first to hear about free content, new releases, cover reveals, sales, and more: www.daniebooks.com/sign-up

You can also join the new reader Facebook group where you can meet other like-minded readers, pick up some exclusive giveaways and stay up-to-date with everything that is happening in my book world. I will have three big announcements in the next couple of months and you don't want to miss them!

You can join the Facebook group here:
https://bit.ly/3Cn5PQJ

MORE FROM DANI ELIAS

Fellside Mountain Rescue Series

Do you want to meet more guys from the Fellside Mountain Rescue Team? Get the rest of the series now:

Discover the world of Fellside Mountain Rescue, where courageous volunteers dedicate their lives to rescuing those lost in the treacherous mountains. But amidst the life-or-death missions, they find themselves facing an equally perilous journey of the heart. In this captivating series, witness the men who risk everything for others also risk it all for love. Join them as they navigate the exhilarating highs and heart-wrenching lows of romance, proving that even in the face of danger, love is a force that cannot be ignored. Prepare to be swept away by the thrilling adventures, passionate connections, and unbreakable bonds forged in the shadow of the mountains.

Alex & Emma: Blossom with Me - Book 1 in the Fellside Mountain Rescue Series

Phil & Christina: <u>Sing with Me</u> – Book 2 in the Fellside Mountain Rescue Series

Nick & Charlotte: <u>Paint with Me</u> – Book 3 in the Fellside Mountain Rescue Series

Chris & Suzie: <u>Climb with Me</u> – Book 4 in the Fellside Mountain Rescue Series

Rob & Olivia: <u>Read with Me</u> – Book 5 in the Fellside Mountain Rescue Series

Tommy & Ella: <u>Build with Me</u> – Book 6 in the Fellside Mountain Rescue Series

Dan & Rose: <u>Wrap Up with Me</u> – Book 7 in the Fellside Mountain Rescue Series

Ryan & Jane: <u>Ride with Me</u> – Book 8 in the Fellside Mountain Rescue Series

Other Books

<u>The Unnatural Habitat of a Cat Lady</u> – **coming soon**

Printed in Great Britain
by Amazon